UNDERGROUND
Tales for London

UNDERGROUND
Tales for London

THE BOROUGH PRESS

The Borough Press
An imprint of HarperCollins*Publishers* Ltd
1 London Bridge Street
London SE1 9GF

www.harpercollins.co.uk

Published by HarperCollins*Publishers* 2018

HarperCollins*Publishers*
1st Floor, Watermarque Building, Ringsend Road,
Dublin 4, Ireland

This paperback edition 2022
1

For London

Contents

Note from the Editor

Born in 1863, the London Underground is a place where everyone comes together, from the city's most wealthy to its homeless, old people, young people, students, residents, visitors . . . five million of us cram into underground carriages every day, to make our way across the city.

It is a place of endless fascination. Lives literally cross over one another. We travel in close proximity across 250 miles of underground track: we mostly stare at our feet, our phones, our newspapers, but occasionally magic can happen – a flirtatious eye caught, a small kindness exchanged. There is occasional tragedy, too, with lives lost, taken, ended.

This short story collection is a celebration of the London Underground, commissioned to mark the opening of the Elizabeth line. The twelve stories – including one memoir – explore the scope of human experience, from family misadventures to spiritual journeys, from the ends of love affairs to those just beginning. Life and death are made manifest, all on the daily commute.

The Mayor of London, Sadiq Khan, said: 'London is open.' This is a city where everyone is welcome, and as these stories demonstrate, the London Underground is the network connecting us all.

ELIZABETH

The Parade

James Smythe

My father, who had been dead for fifteen years, was the last person to board the train. I had that singular sensation of, when looking at a crowd, being able to pick out the one face that meant something to me, to home in on it, to see every detail of it. It was my father, as if he had just been down to the shop and then returned, rather than having succumbed – that's the word that the doctor used, when they called me to visit him: *succumbed* – to his death the way that he did.

But, of course, it wasn't him. It was another man, with a suit like his and a coat like his, brushing around his knees even in the middle of the summer; only this man wasn't dead. His face wasn't as sallow and pallid as my father's, at the end. He took his hat off, and I saw his face. The insides of the hat, so different to my father's; which, I was convinced, held some secrets of the universe, because he would gaze into them when searching for moments of pause, and I would try to distract him. I stared at this man, and he met my eyes, and we smiled, because that's what you do when something is mutually embarrassing. I looked away, then, to the platform; and the most striking memory, of my father, his actual suit and coat, leading me through the station one day when I was small. Holding my hand, guiding me, taking me someplace; I forget where. His hand, folded over mine, so large it swaddled it; and the warmth of it, on my child-thin knuckles.

'Come with me,' he said, as if that was all.

And then, snap, to reality, to the actual then: the light lurch of the train as we left Liverpool Street, leaving Alex's flat for the last time; my rucksack, a bag with my entire life crammed into it, between my knees. The woman opposite me typing on her phone; the man next to me with a script, learning lines, his lips mouthing the words with almost silent sibilance; another woman with a novel, the cover folded backwards, just a tease of a glimpse of what she's reading. For one year of my life, as a challenge, everything that I read was a suggestion from other readers on the underground: the covers acting as part of the lure, solidified by the intensity of the reader's face as they tried to turn as many pages as they could before their stop. I tried to see the woman's book, then, a cover of delicately painted art, but she kept it clenched. I wished that I could have known, because she was so intent that I wanted nothing more than to read it. People on all sides, all living their lives.

The comfort of feeling hemmed in; even if just a little.

I shut my eyes and leaned back. The new trains rattle less than the old. Less of a rocking sensation; somehow both more and less comforting, at the exact same time.

I heard a flapping that I was sure was a pigeon, somehow make its way into the carriage. They do that: they peck their way into stations, down escalators, onto platforms, into lunches. I pictured it, moving down the carriage; head bobbing, inquisitive, nudging crumbs and leaves along the line of the door. And then my phone trilled in my pocket, cutting through the flapping; leaving that noise gone, and no sign of the bird.

A message, from Alex:

I'm sorry. Fly safely. X

I deleted it. Didn't just turn off the screen, act as if it weren't there, but I deleted it. The faff of endless menus, of attempting to discover a way to remove that message, to purge it, while leaving the previous messages – *I can't wait to see you; I thought of you today* – even though, perhaps, those were lies, since no choice such as his gets made so rashly. And I saw my hands – my knuckles, more wrinkled and drawn than I remembered them being, as if I hadn't actually looked at them in the longest time, and time itself had cheated me of whatever near-muscular form I thought that my knuckles once had – and I realized how old I suddenly was. A tidal wave of time, washing over everything, swallowing it whole.

My father had died fifteen years earlier. He had been eighty-five, and old with it; a curmudgeon in a chair at Christmas, paper crown still folded on his placemat, Whisky Mac in hand regardless of what the rest of us were drinking. The man in the crowd reminded me far more of my father when I had been young, still hat and coat and briefcase and a complicit understanding that he was my hero; and I, in some way, maybe was his.

Then, of course, time and life interrupt; and we were at odds. When his father – my grandfather – died, I remember him telling me that he was sad that he never got a chance to say the things that he wanted to say. The gulf between them; the pain.

I told myself that history wouldn't repeat; except, of course, that's the nature of history. Inescapably cyclic.

Farringdon, and the electric slide of the doors that, when I was a child, on another line before this one even existed, used to *hiss* their pleasure at being opened. A girl got on. Ten, or eleven, and dressed for some sort of event: you can see them around at weekends, as superheroes or movie stars. This girl was wearing a bonnet, a Victorian child-heroine writ large. She apologized with her eyes, and she sat next to me. Bunched her skirts up. I folded my body as small as I could, in the space, and she smiled at me. And we left Farringdon, this part of the city that's so old, so well worn; and in the tunnel, in the dark, I saw myself reflected in the window. My face, but somehow barely recognizable. The thump of the dark tunnel outside, seemingly endless, as if leaving the carriage and wading through the black might lead to some parallel world.

'Pardon my intrusion,' a still, small voice said. From the young lady. 'You're Gregory Abbey, aren't you?'

I had a moment where I wondered if there was any chance she'd read one of my novels, but I doubted it – she was not the target audience, if such a thing even existed – and *yet*. Perhaps she was one of Alexander's nieces. He had enough of them, faces that blended in amongst a parade of introductions: *this is my friend, Gregory.*

A lie, a lie, a barely formed truth.

'I'm sorry, but I don't remember you,' I said.

'I'm Alice,' she said. She held her hand out, to shake mine; and mine enveloped hers, a gnarled root swamping soft willow. 'Do you remember me? It has been a while.'

I felt myself spiralling. Shut my eyes, a blink that lasted a count of one, nothing more; and I remembered her. I remembered a photograph that my grandmother herself had shown me, of the day that she had her picture taken. And this was her, my grandmother, Alice Abbey; and she was sitting in front of me.

'Are you real?' I asked her, and she laughed. She didn't answer; which, in itself, is an answer, of sorts. 'Why are you so young? When I last saw you, you were an old woman.'

'Wouldn't you rather look like this, if you could?'

'What are you doing here?' I wondered how loud my voice was; how loud you should be, when speaking to somebody who was meant to be long dead.

'I'm here because you are. I used to ride this stretch,' she said. 'The tunnels don't change, you know.' She smiled. Kicked her feet, which scuffed along the floor.

'But why?' I asked her.

'Because today is when you're going to die,' she told me. 'And this is what happens when you do.'

My dying father's bedside was a strange affair. He was in a hospice, because there was no other way to make sure that he was actually cared for, not the half-arsed care that comes from having one eye on a dying man and another on the food you're burning, the love you're losing, the television you're missing. He wasn't happy, because he wanted me to take him in. But I had Alexander. I told him, then, when he asked why he couldn't move in with me. He said, 'You don't have a wife, you don't have children.'

I told him. He told me not to visit him any more.

The only time I made it through the doors was at the very end. The care workers apologized to me on his behalf. They had seen me sit, and wait, and ask – *beg* – to be let inside; and he had spat at them in proxy for me, this bitter old man.

I watched him die, and he looked at me before he did, too weak to say anything.

He succumbed, and neither of us said what we probably needed to say.

In his box, given to me after he passed, I found his hat. I stared inside it for hours, waiting to see if it would give itself up to me. Give him up to me; but nothing.

'Do you feel it?' Alice asked me. 'How close you are?' My hand instinctively went to my head, to the scar that Alex once remarked was shaped like a suspicious eye. 'They said that I have six months,' I replied, 'but I'm going to Amsterdam, where they have treatments to try . . .' My voice, trailing off, rang in my own ears.

'It's today,' Alice said. Her smile was sympathetic. I looked at the window, the reflection, because I wanted to see what my own face was doing. 'I'm sorry,' she said.

'It's fine,' I replied.

She positively beamed. 'Good. There's some people here who would love to see you.'

The doors opened at Tottenham Court Road. I remembered being here when I was a young man: being brought to Old Compton Street by a friend, to a world where everything felt permitted, and nothing was as I told myself it was. He said, 'You're not true to yourself,' and I suppose that wasn't wrong.

Through the doors, then, the people came. A bustle of them, of tourists and half-termers and commuters, and a busker, singing some old song; and Ronnie, in the middle of them all. That self-same friend, his eyes their almost-iridescent purple shimmer, his smile a spread of honest warmth.

'I can't believe it,' I said.

'Jesus,' he said, 'Greggy! What a delight!' He embraced me, elbows into the other passengers – he was never one to care for what others thought of him, and his celebration was stronger than the personal space of anybody else in the carriage – and pulled me tight. 'Look at you! You look good, considering.'

'And you,' I stammered. Our *considerings* were aligned: I might have been dying, but he had already been dead for going on forty years.

He sat opposite me, his long limbs extended then snapped back, arms folded and legs crossed. 'This is a bit fancy, isn't it?' He looked down the carriage. 'I remember when this was all fields.' A joke; and a grin so delightful that I almost forgot the strangeness of his being there.

'Yes,' I replied, because I didn't have any other words.

'You got old,' he said. Matter-of-fact. 'Still, only as old as you feel.' I remembered him then, in that moment, as he was when he died: gaunt. Not the same as my father, because one was sunken, the other collapsing. A vital difference. I wondered: would I sink? Or would I collapse? Was that what I was doing at that exact moment? 'I knew I'd get here first.' A glint in his eye. 'You lazy shit, taking your time over something so important. I always said that you were a little behind.' Bond Street, and the squash of people, suitcases and children tightly gripping hands.

'Don't think I'm rude,' I said, 'but I have to ask: why are you here?'

They looked at each other, as if the answer should be obvious; and they smiled, because they were in on a private joke that I most definitely was not.

'Think of this as a parade,' Alice said. 'A farewell and mind your way.'

'Death doesn't need to be as dour as the world would have it. We're here to celebrate with you.'

'And what if I don't want to die?' I asked. 'What happens then?'

'You don't have a choice,' Ronnie said.

The train pulled in to Paddington. I waited, for a moment, and then—

I was gone, from my seat, to the platform, rucksack strap gripped in my hand; my worn old knuckles white with the force of my hold. And the doors hushed shut behind me, and I turned to see Alice and Ronnie staring through the glass; and I said, out loud, 'I am not dying today,' and I walked along the platform, watched until the train moved out of sight. 'Not today,' as I sat on a bench. Put my hand to my head, and swore I could feel something under the skin, under the bone, beating alongside my pulse.

Alex drove me to my first appointment, at University College Hospital, back when my illness was nothing more than a persistent headache and an elevated blood-cell count. He sat in the car and said, 'I'll wait here for you.' And I should have known then, really. Because so much with him was, *Let's not make a big deal out of this.*

As I was led through to the test chamber, they asked if I was alone. I told them, 'My partner's in the car,' and they said, each nurse with a slightly different inflection, 'They can come inside, you know,' and I replied, 'Oh, he prefers it.' As if that was justification. Each nurse their own version of a consolatory nod.

'It's hard on the loved ones,' that's what one of the nurses said to me, later; when the prognosis was dealt, and I was reeling, and Alex wasn't with me.

'Yes,' I said, placid as you like; because I didn't want to say, well how do you think it feels to be here alone?

That day, when I got home, my head shaven, hat perched defiantly on my smooth, round skull, he told me that he had spoken to his ex-wife; that they had more to sort out, regarding their children, their house, their possessions.

He asked me if I minded him going to see her.

'Of course not,' I told him. Why would I mind?

I rode the city, the length and breadth of it. I went to whichever line would take me. Every line, every length. Every destination, every station with their shared darknesses in the tunnels, running off for as long as you can imagine; this intricate webbing, underneath the city – *my* city – that links everything, every*place* together. To Pinner, to my old flat, bought when I was in my fifties, the fifth floor of a block that felt craningly high even at only six floors, all vulgar Eighties carpets and wooden kitchen, but so very, very mine; to Kensington, to Alice's house, remembered briefly from when I was a child and she, most definitely, was not, but after the war and she had money and my mother telling me to not touch *anything*; to Hackney, where I lived in the years before it was trendy to say that you lived there, when it really was council terraces and warehouses that couldn't even dream of being turned into communes; to Richmond, to the bars that felt like a part of me when nowhere else was open, where I sat and drank quietly, waiting to be noticed; and to the bookshops at the lower end of Soho, no longer hiding their content in blank covers, smuggled out in my teenaged pockets, no longer hiding anything at all.

I went to all of these places, and yet to none of them; I remembered them all perfectly, a lifetime in just the blink of my eyes; just as people said happened. A flash, so bright in that extended moment as to be almost entirely blinding.

I met Alex when he was already lying to his wife. A friend of mine that I knew online told me about an app, and he explained how to install it onto my phone, and from there I met Alex. He was ten years younger than I was, but he spoke about time as if he was some sort of master of it: the things that he had done, the people he had known, the life he had lived. He had two children, but he never spoke about them and didn't want me to either, as if my saying their names might somehow alert them to my existence. He had a wife, whose name I was allowed to say, but only in a way that suggested I was appreciative of the pain he was enduring by staying with her. 'Oh, Deborah wouldn't understand,' he would moan, hyphenating every syllable with his breath for some sort of extreme emphasis. 'She's known about my dalliances before, but this?' He stroked my arm. 'This love? She wouldn't understand *that*.'

We met in bars on the ground floors of hotels, and then occasionally in restaurants adjacent to those bars. A few times, his wife was away, and we went to his house, where we slept in the guest bedroom, on an undressed mattress and under a naked duvet, in case his wife wondered why the master bedsheets had been changed.

He never came to visit me; I always went to visit him. He left his wife when she caught us one day. Or she left him, I was never sure. I bought my flat, and he bought his, near Liverpool Street. He told me that it was too soon for us to cohabit. 'Besides,' he said, 'are you sure that you want everybody to talk?'

When, eventually, I told him my prognosis, his face was perfectly still for a while, until his eyebrow raised, and he said, 'What a shame.'

As if there was ever a future for us, at all.

O n the platform, at Paddington. Waiting for the purple trains, at the doors, perfectly aligned to the opening of the carriages. The people, crowding, with their bags, their lovers, their pasts and futures; every part of human life somehow finding its way to that platform. I watched as train after train passed through the station.

'Are you OK, sir?' A woman in a uniform, a tabard, smiling at me. I smiled back.

'I'm overwhelmed, that's all.'

'London can do that,' she replied. She looked at my over-filled rucksack, the mark of a visitor. 'You here for a holiday?'

'No. I'm leaving,' I said.

She smiled again. She had a lovely smile. Warm, kind. Reminded me of my mother. 'Let me know if you need anything, OK?'

I stood as she walked off, and I made my way to the marked area of the platform, by the glass doors. Being on a platform would once tousle every part of you as the train rushed towards you; but that time, it was just there.

The doors opened, and there she was: my mother.

Her name was Elizabeth. Betty, she called herself, because – in her words – 'I'm not exactly the Queen, now, am I?'

Ronnie laughed, from his seat. 'I told you he'd be back. Didn't I tell you?'

My mother opened her arms, and I sank into them.

Alice told me about the route she used to take. 'My whole life,' she said, 'this run. This line, these tunnels, they've existed for so long. Not these *exact* tunnels, but adjacent is sometimes the same as the original, don't you think?' The train stopped, and people disembarked, and more boarded. Each time I stared, to see the faces and hear the voices.

'Nothing beats the original,' my old tutor, Sean, said, 'though God knows this city tries: constantly self-imitating.' Sean died of old age, a peaceful passing that made those of us at his funeral somehow envious: his was, we agreed, as if we were all cricketers, a good innings.

'You don't like London,' I said to him, almost under my

breath, a phrase I had recited a hundred times or more in the years that I knew him.

'And you blame him?' My cousin, Vanessa. Long hours spent playing in Alice's garden, when she was in her middle age, and Vanessa and I were, for a time, all each other had. Vanessa took scissors to her own wrists, but those scars weren't visible: in that carriage, she was in her twenties, footloose and free of those fancies that people seem so eager to be free of.

'Not everybody feels like you do, you know.' Arnold, the first boy I ever loved, cancer of the insides, a spread that lost all track of its origin point.

'And not everybody is quite so contentious.' Samir, from the school I once taught in, while trying to make ends meet between novels. Colleague, first reader, friend, infection that rendered him first slightly stilled, then completely static.

'Don't remember Gregory much, then, I take it?' Adelle, agent, dedicated smoker who overcame the odds of the smoker's lot and died, elderly, in a crash.

'As much as I need to,' Ronnie said. Cutting through them all. Ronnie, who died because – as he said in the letter that he left his friends, which we all gathered around to read in the week following his death – he loved too much. His smile was pervasive, able to somehow commit to whatever situation we found ourselves in: that same smile, somehow consistently appropriate. Even then, with my impending.

I pulled him to one side. 'How did you deal with this?' I asked.

'The parade? I decided that everything's a parade now. One big to-do.'

We left the city, or the innards of the city. The part that feels as though it's inescapable when you're inside it, and then so alluring as to be almost unreachable when you're not. The built-up gave way to the suburbs, the built-down: two-storeys, bungalows, flats above shops. Comfort and ease; the love handles of my city.

A memory, of Alex poking my sides, before I got ill. Telling me, 'Well, this is a new addition.' My stomach, his finger sinking into pink flesh. 'Nobody told me we were expecting.'

'I don't know why you stayed with him,' Ronnie said, reading my mind.

'I didn't ask you,' I said. Maybe I spat my words, defensive, because Ronnie looked affronted; but still, his lovely smile essentially formed his face for itself.

'You lived out here, didn't you?' he asked me.

'Once. You didn't.'

'Thank God. I died before I could pretend that I wanted to.' Snark, smirk.

'I did actually want to, you know.'

'You didn't know what you wanted.' His smile changed. Have you ever seen somebody who looks so happy, suddenly so sad? Or maybe not sad, but withdrawn; understanding, empathic. 'It's funny, this. Leaving somewhere. Moving on. The past, going into a place you haven't been yet.'

The train stopped. Hayes and Harlington. Last stop before Heathrow.

Ronnie looked to the doors. My father, definitely him this time, standing there. In the hat that he used to wear, the perfectly pressed suit. His lip a line, a crease, in an otherwise creaseless face.

'I'll leave you two alone,' Ronnie said. He squeezed my arm, near my wrist; and Alice waved at me, and my mother kissed my cheek. Everybody else faded away, until there was just me and him, him and me, in this carriage, thundering past the houses, on its way.

'I lived in a house near here,' I said to him. He sat opposite me, and he did that affectation with his trousers: hitching them slightly, so that they didn't catch on his socks; so that a glimpse of his ankles could be seen, below the braces on his socks. 'The first time that I moved in with somebody, it was here.'

'Nice enough area,' he said. 'I remember coming here when you were a kid. There was a shop. For your models.' I used to build Airfix models. A Sopwith Camel with my grandfather, who saw them during the war. Glue on my fingers, and I would peel it off in what felt like sheets. My father watching us, somehow envious of the relationship I had with him. I didn't know who he was more jealous of. 'How long's this line been open, then?'

'A year or so,' I replied. He nodded. Information, not good or bad; just useful. 'I loved him,' I said. My father didn't blink.

A pause, as pregnant as any I have ever experienced.

'It's different,' he finally said. 'Than what you expect.'

'What is?'

'Where you're going.' He moved to stare out of the window, pushing his face to the glass so that he could see along the track as we followed a bend.

'Did you have this?'

'Everybody has this.'

'So who was at yours?' I felt petulant. As if, if I kept him talking, maybe I could stay alive for longer. Maybe I could prolong the inevitable; the succumbing.

'Oh, you know. Your Uncle Jackie, he was there. My

friends. Some of the boys from the Rose.' He took his hat off. His hair a fine dusting. 'Your grandfather.'

'What did he say to you?'

He examined the insides of his hat. All the secrets of life, in there. 'He said that he didn't care what we'd never spoken about. He said that it didn't matter, in the end.' He stood up. I distinctly remember it: his standing as punctuation, perfectly timed with the train's arrival; the slowing, the coasting, towards the airport's station. 'That's what I would say, Gregory. I've read your books. I like to think that I know the measure of you.' The train stopped in a tunnel, briefly. In the dark, waiting for a platform; for an ending. Good to know that some things never change. 'We should go,' he said.

'I don't know how I feel,' I told him.

'I don't think you *should* know.'

I followed him, off the train, and to the platform. Through the windows, I could see something ill-defined: a person, a man, left on the train. Sitting very still in his seat, waiting to be found. And when that body was found, it would cause a delay. I felt guilty then, in that British way that we feel guilt for our actions altering the lives of those we don't know; but then the trains would run to schedule again, and all would be well.

Alex would be called to identify, because there was only

really one number in the body's telephone that mattered; and he would stand back, hand over mouth. Surprised, but not surprised. He would say that I was a friend of his, I'm sure.

It didn't matter.

One day, he would die: and he would have his own parade. His own things left unsaid; his own regrets.

I wondered if I would be called upon to visit him; and if I would, then, refuse.

My father's stride, through the station, towards the exit. I watched him, slightly behind. I felt myself younger, then; in my twenties. Scared, afraid. My hands in my pockets.

He turned to look at me. 'There he is,' he said, nodding. His thin mouth a satisfied smile. 'There he is.' He reached his hand out for me, and, 'Come with me.'

I slipped mine – so young again, the knuckles smooth, taut – into his; and I succumbed, to a mutual whatever.

DISTRICT

Blackfriars

Matthew Plampin

4 January 1892

The president arrived in the lobby at a brisk pace, his boot heels clacking down the marble staircase. He was exactly as he'd been described: tall and uncommonly thin, about sixty years old, with a broad forehead and a silvery, scrupulously neat beard. His suit was black, cut close and worn with a frilled dress shirt, an eccentric touch that somehow increased the severity of the overall effect. The clerk at the desk – who'd been eyeing Merrill from time to time, as if suspecting that he might try to pocket an inkwell – was off his stool immediately, retrieving coats and hats from a small chamber beside the doors. Merrill rose to his feet, doing his best to appear alert and useful. Uncle Bob, descending a few feet behind the president, gave him a weary look.

'This is James Merrill, Mr Leyland,' he said. 'My nephew.'

The clerk helped the president into a black overcoat,

which was buttoned up to the neck, and then handed over a spotless black topper. After fitting this carefully on his head, the president turned towards Merrill for a momentary appraisal. There was an odd blankness about his eyes, and when he spoke his voice was devoid of interest.

'He dresses well.'

Uncle Bob accepted his own coat and shrugged it on. 'Dressing,' he replied, 'Merrill can do.'

Before joining the National Telephone Company Uncle Bob had been an officer of infantry, ranking somewhere in the middle, and you could see it in him now – that deep-dyed regard for hierarchy that soldiers were prone to have. Attending on this Mr Leyland, he was every inch the loyal lieutenant, moving aside smartly as the president made for the doors. Only then did Merrill realize that someone else had come down with them, another junior like himself; this man was older, though, thirty-five at least, blond-whiskered and bordering upon portliness.

'I am Mr Carlens,' he said, skirting the desk to fetch a grey coat and bowler. 'Mr Leyland's private secretary.'

Was that condescension in Mr Carlens' expression – a shade of scorn, even? Merrill could hardly blame him if it was. His situation was plain enough, there for anyone to divine: that stale story of hapless youth, surrendered to an upstanding family elder for correction and supplied with an unearned career in business for which he was proving markedly ill-suited. Merrill wasn't at all proud of this. There were days, in truth, when he could scarcely bear the sight of his own reflection.

The two juniors went out into the dull January evening. Uncle Bob had been summoned to Leyland's office in the City only an hour or so before, to escort him back to the telephone company's premises on Temple Lane. No cab was being called, however, nor was there any sign of the grand private carriage that the president was said to keep on hand both day and night. Merrill saw that Leyland and Uncle Bob had turned to the left, and were following the crowds that tramped down towards Cannon Street.

'Are we not—' he began. 'Forgive me, Mr Carlens, but isn't there a—'

'Mr Leyland wishes to take the underground.'

Merrill managed to contain his disbelief – merely to nod, as an unquestioning subordinate should do. Frederick Richards Leyland was, without doubt or exception, the richest man in England. Some at the telephone company claimed that by the end of that year he would be the richest man alive. He had millions in the bank. Carriages and country houses. A Kensington mansion in which the finest modern paintings were displayed like stamps in an album.

'This surprises you,' Carlens observed.

They started out in pursuit of their employers. Merrill watched the president's pristine topper shimmer as it passed beneath a street lamp. 'I haven't been with the company very long, Mr Carlens. There is much I do not—'

'It is true that Mr Leyland is averse to crowds, generally speaking.' The private secretary lowered his voice; Merrill sensed that he relished his position at the president's side and the insights it permitted. 'There are a good number who conduct their business hereabouts whom he would not care to meet. Who might well seize upon the chance to speak with him.' Carlens surveyed the hundreds streaming around them: this world of men, emptying out at the day's end, marching off to stations and omnibus stands. 'The chances are slight, of course – but still, eyes peeled, eh?'

Cannon Street was broad and busy, bending away to the right; beyond the buildings was a clipped view of St Paul's, the half-dome almost lost in the dark, starless sky. Directly ahead, among the bright shop fronts, a steady procession of people was disappearing between a stationer's and an optician's, down a tiled stairway into the underground. Merrill knew the District line with regrettable intimacy. It was an unchanging fact of his existence, ridden from Earl's Court to Temple and back again: an hour eaten out of each and every day. Routine had numbed him to the point where he didn't usually notice how it was. That evening, though, as he left the street and hurried onto the steps, he saw it as the president must surely be seeing it. The cracked and grubby tiles. The cement floor, littered with flattened cigarette ends and scraps of paper. And the blasted *smoke*, that gritty, metallic smell, tobacco and coal intermingled, hazing the air and making the subterranean ticket hall yet dingier.

The president and Uncle Bob had stopped in the middle of this low-ceilinged atrium, a pair of ill-matched rocks lodged in the ceaseless flow of commuters. Uncle Bob, clearly uncomfortable, was tugging at his grizzled moustache. Leyland was taking in his surroundings with evident distaste, coughing genteelly in the muddy atmosphere.

'Tickets, Merrill,' said Uncle Bob, as if this was obvious and really should have been guessed. 'First class, back to Temple.'

Chastened, Merrill went to join the queue. Five windows were open at the office, and perhaps two hundred people presently trying to pay. He could only choose a line and stand in it. Around him was a dense, lulling murmur, several dozen shifting conversations, their words blurring together. His thoughts wandered to a common in high summer, near a friend's house at Richmond; to Emily in her blouse and boater, and that song they'd all sung together: *Within the musk-rose bower, I watch, pale flower of love, for thee . . .*

'Louse!' someone shouted.

Merrill turned sharply to see a man, a perfectly ordinary-looking man in a blue sack coat, standing up close before the president and yelling in his face.

'Louse,' he repeated. 'Villain – wrecker!'

A companion was trying to restrain him. Carlens strode forward to assist, planting a hand on the shouting fellow's chest and gesticulating angrily, ordering him away. Uncle Bob was colouring, huffing something under his breath, outraged on their master's behalf – for Leyland himself seemed entirely unmoved. He was looking across the concourse as if this man in the blue sack coat simply didn't exist. Seeing he would get no response, the assailant barked 'wrecker' for a second time, and asked the president loudly if he understood at all what he had done, what he had destroyed; and then he stalked off furiously towards the street.

Merrill returned his gaze to the ticket office. Not *that* slight a chance then, Mr Carlens! he thought. He wondered what lay behind this little confrontation. There was much talk about Frederick Leyland over at Temple Lane. President of the National Telephone Company, Merrill had learned, was but one of his positions. Leyland was also a major figure in electricity, having a sizeable stake in Edison, and a ship-broker with a huge transatlantic fleet. This was the origin of his wealth, in fact, numbering upward of thirty steamers.

The very idea of it boggled the mind. It was said that his ambition knew no boundary or scruple – that the shipping company up in Liverpool had been won through the betrayal of his mentor, and he had conducted himself ever since with absolute ruthlessness, leaving a trail of crushed competitors in his wake. And every company director bested in negotiations and lawyerly manoeuvrings had an operation behind him – sales merchants and accountants and clerks, each with his wife, his infants, his poorly parents. A lot of livelihoods. A lot of lives.

The tickets were purchased distractedly, Merrill almost forgetting to buy first class. It was hardly his habit. Uncle Bob was talking with determination about some subject or other, in order to dispel any lingering unpleasantness. The four men started down the central staircase to the platforms. Merrill was regarding Leyland more closely than ever, studying the precise arrangement of the hair above his collar, which had the look of having been trimmed that same morning. A warm, dirty wind gusted up to meet them. The president coughed once more, against his hand.

'Already, Colonel,' he remarked to Uncle Bob in his detached manner, 'I believe you can see quite clearly where the problem lies.'

They were attracting notice. You couldn't fail to spot it; Leyland was being recognized. Merrill recalled the more salacious rumours that bubbled through the Temple Lane offices – rumours that claimed it was not merely companies their president had wrecked. This was a man with a great appetite for women, as brimming with lust as he was empty of passion, and with the means to make any obstacle to his desires vanish; and unburdened, furthermore, by any guilt or self-reflection upon the matter.

'He doesn't care who knows about his activities,' one especially talkative junior surveyor had confided, equal parts scandalized and impressed, over an after-hours mug of porter. 'It doesn't trouble him a jot.'

Such behaviour, the surveyor had continued, had naturally added to the number of Leyland's foes. There had been a wife at one point, a beautiful woman, well-liked and decent, who was driven out in the coldest, cruellest fashion. Leyland's essential nature was one that could not help but repel. Over the years he had suffered vicious ruptures with everyone from his doctor to his decorator.

'His *decorator*?'

'That was a while ago now. A dreadful to-do. The plan for his dining room went awry, you see, and they disagreed over the bill. Yankee fellow it was, a Mr Whistler. Friend of the wife's as well. It's said that Leyland threatened to take him out and whip him in the street.'

Merrill followed art. It was one of the reasons for his

family's concern. 'You mean *James* Whistler, the artist?' he'd asked. 'The painter of nocturnes, who has a show coming at the Goupil Gallery?'

This had met only with a shrug.

The party headed onto the westbound platform. It was filled with City men, standing alone mostly, buried in their newspapers or simply staring at their shoes. The air was yet more turbid than in the concourse. Spherical lamps hung at intervals along the tiled ceiling, but the smoke soaked up their light, obscuring them to the point where the furthest were reduced to fogged, yellowish smears. Weaving between the other passengers, Leyland led them beneath the large, plain clock that hung at the platform's midpoint. Then he went to the edge and beckoned for Uncle Bob to join him. They began pointing down at the tracks, conversing in low, purposeful tones.

Carlens stayed in the middle of the platform, monitoring those nearby – a couple of whom were directing sidelong looks at the president.

Merrill stood next to him. 'Train shouldn't be more than a minute or two.'

The private secretary wasn't listening. 'You see now,' he said, nodding towards Leyland, 'what this is about.'

Merrill kept quiet.

'Electricity,' Carlens enlarged. 'Or rather *electrification*.

Mr Leyland is always thinking of the future. You know of his share in the Edison company? He sees this line being powered that way, and lit that way too. He sees telephones connecting the stations – connecting the platforms and the offices. Vast improvements, Mr Merrill. Vast indeed.'

Merrill crossed his arms, frowning slightly as if in contemplation. He was impressed, rather to his annoyance, and stung by a sudden and profound sense of inadequacy. He simply could not think in these terms. His grand idea, the sum of his life's ambition, was that he might write for the stage – and that was receding into the distance at a rate of knots. Now he sought chiefly to keep his damned family at bay, and escape the censure of Uncle Bob. This long-limbed black-clad rake, so sinister and ridiculous, had plainly wrought more than his share of harm – but he had *vision*. It was the only word. Leyland saw the shape of things to come, and the practical changes that would affect the progress of cities. Of entire nations.

'There's gold down here,' Carlens went on, satisfied by Merrill's reaction, 'in these wretched tunnels. Mr Leyland perceives it clearly. A rich seam of it. He changed shipping, you know, changed it for good, and now he'll change the underground. Make his fortune all over again, I shouldn't wonder.'

'And the boon for London will be incalculable,' Merrill

added. 'I mean to say, Mr Leyland will – well, he will be doing the people of this city an enormous service.'

Carlens was eyeing him with a certain pity, as if noting a lack. He inclined his grey bowler in acknowledgement. 'Quite so.'

A high-pitched whistle sounded off to the right, and light broke around a corner of the tunnel. A few seconds later the squat, sooty locomotive heaved itself into the station, sending banks of smoke and steam rolling through the still mistiness of the platform. Its wheezing chugs and the prolonged whine of its brakes made any further conversation impossible. Leyland and Uncle Bob stepped back, for a moment reduced to silhouettes; then Uncle Bob went after one of the leading carriages, following it a few yards along the platform before opening a door for the president. As the juniors hurried up behind them, Merrill noticed the '1's stencilled on the carriage's other doors: first class. There was less competition for seats here, most of those out on the platform making for the other, inferior sections of the train. They had a compartment to themselves – unheard of in second or third class at this time on a Monday. Merrill embarked last and took a place on the left, directly inside, facing Carlens. The furnishings, he noticed, were a little fresher and better made; the upholstered bench seats a few inches further apart. The smell was the same, though:

tobacco ash and gas, and the ever-present smoke. He reached over to close the door.

There was a shout from the platform guard and the blast of a pea whistle, and the underground train pulled from the station. Once they were out in the tunnel, Uncle Bob asked Leyland about the City and South London Railway, one of the new, deep-running lines, which had been using electric traction locomotives for over a year. Leyland was disdainful. It was a ramshackle operation, he replied, unreliable and poorly implemented. The generators barely provided sufficient power for the engines – there was nothing left for lighting or—

This bout of coughing seemed to catch him unawares. It sounded different, constricted, as if his throat was tightening. The carriage swayed upon the track; the single gas fitting hissed softly above them. Merrill looked away into the inky sheen of the window, just as the train arrived at Mansion House. The platform here was as busy as the one at Cannon Street. Two well-fed managerial types advanced on their compartment. Carlens held the handle, keeping them out, waving them on with his other hand. The gentlemen persisted, but the private secretary held firm. Eventually the whistle blew, and with shakes of the head they went to board elsewhere.

'Are you well, sir?' asked Uncle Bob.

'Quite well,' Leyland answered hoarsely, between coughs. 'It will pass.'

The train continued westwards. Recovering himself, the president addressed Uncle Bob, sketching the outlines of a new concern that would be able to take full advantage of this opportunity he had detected. Merrill gathered that it would be founded on the Edison company, which would be bought out, gulped down whole, much as Leyland had done with his shipping firm in Liverpool.

'Edison can be improved,' he said. 'Expanded. I'm convinced of that. This underground railway will only grow, Colonel, and every last foot of it will require electrification.'

Uncle Bob was enthusiastic. With Leyland presiding, he said, it would surely work; as with so much in business, the vital elements would be leadership and sheer force of will, and the president possessed both of these in abundance. On and on he went. Merrill began to loathe him a little for his sycophancy.

Leyland made a sound, as if in interjection, raising one of his bony hands suddenly from his lap. Uncle Bob came to an obedient halt. They all waited patiently to see what comment or insight he might offer.

Nothing came. The raised hand began to tremble, Leyland's strange, blank eyes popping wide. Merrill glanced over at Uncle Bob. He was sitting forward, hands on his knees like Ingres' *Monsieur Bertin*, his ruddy face hidden in the shadow of his hat brim – plainly concerned, yet reluctant to act in case this prompted his master's ire. Leyland spoke very faintly; a squeal of steel from somewhere below drowned out his voice.

'Pardon me, Mr Leyland?' said Uncle Bob. 'What was that, sir?'

'I can't breathe,' Leyland whispered.

Uncle Bob was off his seat at once, propriety and reserve forgotten, reaching for the president's neck – then exclaiming in frustration, tearing the gloves from his hands, unbuttoning Leyland's overcoat down to the middle of his chest. Carlens leapt to his feet, and Merrill as well, their hats bumping against the compartment roof, although there was nothing at all that either could do. Beyond Uncle Bob's shoulder, Merrill could see the president pulling feebly at the frills that lined his shirt front, attempting to undo his collar.

Leyland managed to inhale, gasping like a man surfacing after a deep dive. He took four more heaving breaths, and nodded to Uncle Bob to indicate respite. The rest of them relaxed a fraction, and were starting to return to their seats when as one they realized that the president was tipping slowly to the side, towards the window. Carlens lunged in to support him. Leyland's head lolled horribly, the topper falling to the floor. Even in the compartment's weak gaslight Merrill could see that he was mortally pale.

'What is this?' asked Carlens. The private secretary's cool urbanity was gone; he sounded fearful. 'Could it – could it be poison?'

Uncle Bob was looking hard across the carriage, to where the lights of the next station were just coming into view. 'His heart,' he said, as the train left the tunnel. 'I've seen it before.'

Elbowing Merrill aside, he went to the door, wrenched down the window and shouted for assistance, his head passing mere inches from the startled crowd that lined the platform. The train shook to a halt. A noise came from the president, a tiny croak, along with the slightest twitching motion. Uncle Bob went back to him. Carlens stepped away and sat opposite. Merrill stood fixed in place, able only to stare.

'Merrill,' Uncle Bob snapped. He hesitated, then softened his tone. 'James. Come here, lad. Help me lift him out.'

Leyland was heavy despite his leanness. Merrill stood behind, his arms around the millionaire's frilled chest, the fellow's shoulder-blades jutting into his thighs. It took a good deal of concentration to edge him through the doorway without knocking his head, which without its topper seemed dreadfully vulnerable and exposed. At the same time, however, Merrill knew that his efforts were merely for show, for there could be little doubt that this was no fainting fit or fleeting ailment. Frederick Leyland was at the point of death, if he had not passed it already. He had no more breath or movement in him.

A station guard was there to meet them, drawn over by Uncle Bob's bellows. Behind him, a number of other passengers stood in a loose semicircle, all craning necks and questioning eyes. Sight of the president stopped the guard mid-query; he turned and attempted to contain the gathering crowd. This great giant of British business was laid there on the underground platform, parallel to the train, as respectfully as they could manage. Uncle Bob set down the legs, then came to help Merrill with the chest and head. Carlens was standing half out of the carriage, his posture slack, robbed of purpose; the black topper, rather dusty now, hung limply in his hands.

The crowd was growing steadily – *a fellow lying dead*, people were saying, *right there by the train!* Merrill moved back. Before long he heard Leyland's name, a shiver of recognition passing through the station, further increasing the interest. They were at Blackfriars. The station was in an open trench, only one level below the street. Its platforms were under cover, but above the trains was the evening sky; the tops of buildings, touched with gaslight; and St Paul's again, from the other side, glimpsed through the rising steam.

Someone was praying. Uncle Bob knelt by the body to put his ear to the president's breastbone, but heard nothing. Merrill put his hands in his pockets, not knowing what else to do with them. He looked off to the platform's end and found himself imagining a multitude – every enemy, living and dead, that Leyland had acquired during the course of his extraordinary, cold-hearted existence, filing down the double staircase. This ethereal company walked in procession between the wrought-iron pillars and drifting clouds of coal smoke, joining the circle pressing in around the dead man. Few showed any sign of grief. Indeed, most were well satisfied, and a few visibly glad; others positively frothed with fury, mouthing curses, ready to spit on the hated figure where it lay. There were the shipping partners from Liverpool, whom Leyland had knifed in the back; the ruined competitors, the discarded mistresses, the man in the blue sack coat from Cannon Street station; the unwanted wife standing quietly dignified, her face behind a veil; even the artist Whistler, who Merrill had once seen caricatured in *Vanity Fair* – a dapper little Yankee with a monocle and a bamboo cane, peering over with grim curiosity.

'James,' said Uncle Bob. 'James, we need to fetch a doctor.'

Merrill blinked; the vision was dispelled. He stared down

at the black legs, sticking out so rigidly. The disquieting whiteness of the face. 'A doctor,' he repeated.

'An examination must be made,' Uncle Bob explained, his voice hushed and urgent. 'A declaration of death. Before we can have him removed from this place.' He pointed towards the exit. 'Quickly, boy. *Go*.'

The road outside the station ran between Ludgate Circus and the mouth of Blackfriars Bridge, and was as clogged with people and traffic as any in London. It was bitterly cold as well, a wintry breeze whipping in from the river. Merrill emerged from the concourse and began to work his way onto the packed pavement. He hadn't the faintest idea where a doctor might be found in Blackfriars at that hour. Out there in the rawness of the open air, however, the last of the underground's grimy heat leaving his clothes, he felt only relief. He looked around him a little dizzily, trying to get his bearings; then he straightened his hat and started off into the city.

CIRCLE

Joanna Cannon

Some people read on the underground. Others push buttons on telephones. I've always been more of a thinker. I'm not one for novels, and I only have a mobile telephone because someone in a shop once talked me into it. Cyril was with me and he went right along with the idea.

'It'll be good for emergencies, Margaret,' he said. 'Stop you from feeling alone.'

Except none of the emergencies I've encountered since has ever benefited from the presence of a telephone, and in all honesty I'm not sure I will ever feel alone again.

There are lots of us on tube trains – the thinkers. If you look hard enough, you can spot us amongst the paperbacks and the newspapers, and the quiet conversation of strangers. We stare at the floor, losing our thoughts in the clutter of other people's feet. We hide our worries in the tired pattern of the seats. We wrap our feelings along the brightly coloured handrails. Nothing is demanded of you on the underground except to wait and stare, suspended in time and place, as life transfers you from one situation to the next. I have always thought a journey was the perfect opportunity to reflect. To think about what comes next. To wait for God to make a decision about why you're there, I suppose.

I enjoy all the different underground services, but the Circle line has always been my favourite. More so now. There's a strange comfort in circles. A reassurance. Although the Circle line isn't a circle any more, of course. A tadpole, Cyril used to call it. 'Look at its little tail,' he'd say and laugh. Gone are the days when you could rotate around the bowels of London uninterrupted. Now, we are all tipped out at Edgware Road and forced to make a decision about ourselves.

Obviously, my decision is very easy.

I just catch the next train and travel all the way back again.

Everything began just after Cyril died. At least, I think it did. It might have been going on for the longest time before then and I didn't notice. We knew Cyril was going to pass away. The consultant told us several times, and in no uncertain terms. *Do you understand what I'm telling you?* he'd say, after every third sentence. *Yes, yes,* we'd say, *we understand.* Perhaps we didn't seem distressed enough. Not quite the right amount of sorrow. I hadn't realized there were guidelines on how to behave when someone is told they are dying, but clearly, we had fallen outside their parameters. Getting upset shrinks a person though, doesn't it? Because once you allow the misery to escape, it takes with it your resolution and your determination and your resilience, and it feeds them all to your problem. Until the problem grows big and fat, and you are left behind, emptied and almost disappeared. Much better to remain logical. To hold onto your strength.

'Everyone dies,' Cyril said, on the journey back from the hospital. 'It's not as though it comes as a surprise, is it? We've known it would happen since the day we were born.'

We were walking home from the tube station, along avenues the estate agent had once described as 'leafy', but which were now unburdened of their charm by an early December evening. Cyril was wearing his old brown lace-ups. Shoes I had begged him to replace for the past two years. I studied them as he walked in front of me along the pavement, and I said to myself, 'He'll never agree to replace them now, will he?' The thought pierced my mind so suddenly, and so deeply, that for a few moments I couldn't remember how to breathe. It's not the big thing that tears you apart, is it? It's all the smaller things that gather at its edges.

'We'll need to go through the box files,' he said. 'Sort out any paperwork.'

'Yes,' I said, 'we will.'

'Tie up any loose ends.'

'Yes,' I said. 'Loose ends.'

I studied his silhouette in a smudge of orange street light. The angle of his trilby. The faint stoop of his shoulders. The way he crooked his left arm ever so slightly, as though he was always waiting for me to join him. I stared at all these things and as I stared, I wondered how long they would remain firm in my memory, and how long it would be before I had to start imagining them instead.

'And of course, we need to make a decision about Jessica.'

He carried on walking as he said the words, sending them back over his shoulder in the casual way one might talk about the weather.

I didn't reply.

Whenever I travel on the underground, the thing that fascinates me most, is below my feet and above my head, countless other people are all doing exactly the same thing, yet each of us is completely unaware of the others' existence. All those ordinary lives held together in the darkness. A puzzle of people. People whose lives are inexorably linked to our own, yet who will always remain invisible to us. I think about them, as I travel the Circle line all day. I search, past the smeared windows coated in the breath of strangers, past the white reflection of my own staring, and I wonder who is out there in the darkness, staring back. Just out of reach.

There's a need for vigilance at the stations, though, so I can't daydream too much. Wood Lane, Latimer Road, Ladbroke Grove, Westbourne Park. I could recite them before I go to sleep, like a small prayer. I never used to notice the names when I was a commuter. I would drift from one station to the next without a second thought, relying on the sway of the carriage and some strange, deep-rooted sense of place to know when I should stand and begin making my way through the wall of people towards the doors. Now I follow the map. Now I silently mouth the place names along with the electronic voice. Since Cyril died, I have the quickened eyes of a tourist.

The consultant was wary of a time frame, but in the end, his caution was pinpoint. Six months. Almost to the week. Those were a strange six months, because when

Cyril first became ill, we spent all our time searching for encouragement. Each evening, we sifted through the events of the day to feed our optimism. Archaeologists of hope. Once we knew he was dying, the treasure hunt was over. We were on a road of inevitability, and no matter how attractive we tried to make the landscape, the certainty of our path made each day seem less fruitful. More of an obligation to get to the other side. It's at times like those you realize it's only really hope that glues everything else together.

As luck would have it, Cyril was reasonably well until the final two weeks. There were days so mundane, we celebrated in the reassurance of their ordinariness. The comfort of small routines, the absence of hospital appointments and doctors who had run out of ideas, the small seed of absurdity that perhaps they had got it all wrong. They hadn't, of course. The drawer spilling with medication told us that. The cheery 'hello' of the Macmillan nurse. Ridiculous things like the best before dates on tins of soup and the day the daffodils finally died away. We tiptoed around the illness for fear it would waken at the sound of our voices and grow larger. On occasion, though, it needed to be mentioned, even if it was indirectly.

'You'll remember where we keep the spare fuses,' he said.

'I will,' I replied.

'And that back door always starts sticking when the weather changes. You just need to push it with your foot. Right at the bottom.'

'I know, Cyril,' I said. 'I know.'

We sorted out the box files. Cyril spent entire mornings at the dining room table, peering over the top of his glasses at pieces of paper, making a decision about each one and putting them all into piles. Keep. Throw Away. Undecided. It felt as though he was going on annual leave, temporarily handing over custody and giving me an opportunity to be solely in charge of our lives for a short while. Except it wouldn't be our lives any more. It would just be mine.

After a few weeks, he finally reached the bottom of the last file. The only things remaining were errant paperclips and receipts so faded, no one would ever know what had been received. It was only at that point he turned to me, took off his glasses and placed them very carefully on the tablecloth.

'We need to tell Jessica,' he said.

I straightened the piles of Keep, Throw Away, Undecided. I gathered up the paperclips. I stared out of the patio doors into the watercolour of a spring lunchtime.

'I don't think there's any need to tell her,' I said. 'Why does she even have to know?'

Cyril pinched at the bridge of his nose, where his

spectacles had left the dent of a morning's work. 'She'll wonder where I am, Margaret.'

'I'll tell her you've gone away,' I said.

Cyril shook his head very slightly.

'I'll tell her you've left me, then. That's it.' I put the paperclips back into a box file. 'That should do the trick.'

Cyril gave a very large sigh. 'She needs to know the truth, Margaret. She's not stupid.'

'No,' I said. 'No, she's not stupid.'

*F*eeble-minded. That was the term they used about Jessica. I was a small child, but I still remember it. Not stupid or thick or backward, but *feeble-minded*. Perhaps in an attempt to make the whole thing sound more elegant. No one's fault. One of those things.

My mother said she always knew Jessica was different as soon as she was born.

'Jessica wasn't like you, Margaret,' she would tell me. 'You were the only baby I had to go by, but I knew there was something wrong, right from the start.'

Jessica was fractious, restless, loud. She refused to be comforted. She wouldn't feed. She wouldn't sleep. She screamed all day and all night. I would lie in bed, fingers pressed into my ears, trying to remember a time when she didn't exist. There didn't seem to be a week when Jessica hadn't succumbed to one infection or another, when she wasn't struggling to swallow, when she wasn't filled with rage.

My parents tried everything. A carousel of specialists in distant rooms. My mother, thick with misery. My father, fingertips barely touching the edges of reason. I don't remember much of the conversations, but I do remember one doctor smiling at my parents across the width of a desk, and saying, 'Why not have another baby? This one really isn't going to bring you very much joy.'

Keep. Throw away. Undecided.

Jessica couldn't speak, but she understood. As she grew, she learned other ways to communicate. Kicks. Bites. Scratches. It would take my mother hours to dress her each morning as I watched from a doorway. There were days my mother painted her face in coats of bright optimism, and other days when she would curl up in the corner of the room and have to be coaxed back into the world again by my father.

When Jessica was five, it was decided she was uneducable. Disabled of the mind. She couldn't be sent to school, and so the education authority thought she should be put into an institution instead. The health authority agreed. My parents, who looked after Jessica every waking minute of her life, and who were the greatest authority of all, were never listened to.

'We fought to keep her at home,' my mother said for years afterwards. 'We fought as hard as we could.'

I never really knew if she was telling me, or telling some past, long-forgotten version of herself.

Jessica was sent away. It was for the best. Everything was for the best. My parents said it to each other. People said it to my parents. Doctors. Friends. Strangers in the street. *For the best* became attached to every sentence, like a quietening balm. A balm that soothes but never heals.

The first place was a sprawl of Victorian melancholy in a far corner of Essex. We travelled there, each Sunday. Whilst everyone else went to church, my parents went to worship at an altar of their own self-loathing. Getting there and back took the best part of a day, and I would stare through the smeared windows of train carriages and watch London ebb and flow, until it was replaced by farms and fields, and the scatter of nameless villages. St Catherine's, it said at the gate. Children's Home for the Mentally Defective. As though all the children inside were small pieces of damaged machinery.

The corridors were lengthy and yellowed. The doors were

all shut. Staff skimmed the edges of distant hallways, but we never saw any other children. You could hear them, though. Echoing around the fancy cornices and the giant cast-iron fireplaces, the smothered sound of unquiet minds. Jessica waited for us in a panelled room. My sister, buttoned into someone else's clothes, because no one wore their own things at St Catherine's. There was a giant cupboard at the far end of each dormitory, and what the staff decided to dress you in was pot luck. All the beautiful outfits my mother had made were walking around on someone else. The four of us sat in a semicircle of matching high-back chairs and stared at each other. My mother would try to hug Jessica. Jessica would squirm away. Then the three of us would leave. It felt like a trip to the Natural History Museum. As though we had been to look at an exhibition no one else knew anything about.

They make documentaries about these places now. Cyril and I watched one. There was a presenter standing in a derelict room, waving his hands around and shouting about asylums. Black and white photographs. The stutter of an old film reel. All those broken lives, all those unheard stories. Except this wasn't just a story. This was my sister.

Cyril was right.

Jessica isn't stupid.

There's little point in starting my day now until the rush hour is over, as London is held static in a charge of elbows and frustration. Cyril and I used to be in the middle of that. We spent years pressed into endless carriages, breathing into the material of strangers' overcoats, standing on the right, living our lives behind yellow lines.

I usually set off from home around ten thirty. That way I can go about my business in peace. I take a packed lunch, because it can get quite expensive going to those little kiosks at the stations. I used to take my knitting, just to pass the time, but I quickly realized you need to have your wits about you to have any chance of success. It's easy to miss someone in a crowded carriage, and you can spend the rest of the day trying to locate them again. I tend to look at people's feet if I've a moment to spare, because it's amazing what you can learn about someone just from their shoes. I try to guess the kind of person they belong to, and when I look up, nine times out of ten I'm right.

The only time I allow myself to daydream, is when we're beneath Hammersmith. I know Jessica is up there somewhere. She has moved many times since the days of St Catherine's. Sheltered. Assisted. Lodge. House. Home. Care. The same situation wrapped up in different words. Victorian panels were swapped for primary coloured walls. High-back chairs for activity rooms and sensory play. She was given a physiotherapist, a nutritionist, an occupational therapist. She even has a speech therapist who managed to find a voice no one had ever heard before. Jessica uses this voice sparingly, words chosen with care and usually released from her mouth one by one. In that way, I think she is probably wiser than the lot of us. Wherever she's lived, though, it's always been the same. She is forever out of sight. In the far corner of hospital grounds, or behind towering hedges, shuttered windows, closed blinds. Hidden away where no one else can see. It was the thing Cyril remarked upon the first time he met her. My parents were long gone, and I had been left to make the pilgrimage alone each Sunday, until Cyril volunteered to go with me.

'Where is it then?' he said.

Jessica had been moved yet again, and we were driving through the edges of Kent, Cyril peering through the passenger window.

'It's not visible from here. It's beyond those trees. Do you see?' I pointed.

'Round the bend,' he said.

'Pardon?' I took my eyes off the road. 'What did you say?'

'It's where the saying comes from. Round the bend. People were housed where no one would ever think to look.'

'Is it true? Did the saying really originate because of that?'

'I don't know.' He shrugged. 'Makes sense though, doesn't it? We only see what's right in front of us, don't we?'

I turned the car into a long driveway. 'I suppose so,' I said.

Jessica loved Cyril. At first, I thought it was because he was someone new to stare at, but she never lost her fascination for him. She moved with us through each decade, but it was always difficult to see her as anything but a child, even though her small body grew hunched and brittle with age, her hair became grey, and upon her face the lines appeared of a life which had never quite been lived.

'Why don't you take her out?' one of the staff would say, seeing how settled she was. 'The park, or for a little drive?'

'I don't think so.' I'd answer quickly, before Cyril had the chance. 'The weather looks a bit unpredictable. Maybe next time.'

If the weather wasn't unpredictable, it would be too hot to sit in a car. Or too cold. The park would be too noisy. Or too quiet. The grass too wet. The air too dry.

Maybe next time.

Jessica would follow the conversation. Her gaze darting between us. Eyes black as jet, just like our mother's.

'The staff take her out all the time, you know?' Cyril said one day, on the drive home. 'The shops. The cinema. She went to the theatre the other week – she loves the theatre.'

'I'm aware of that,' I said.

'So, why is it never next time?'

I stared at the traffic lights as we waited. I didn't reply.

'Why do you want to keep her hidden away? Are you ashamed?'

I turned to him and stared. 'She's my sister. Of course I'm not ashamed! Just because we're married doesn't give you the right to insult me left, right and centre.'

'I'm not insulting you, Margaret. I'm just trying to get to the bottom of it.'

The thing Cyril didn't realize, was that I was trying to get to the bottom of it too.

The staff stopped asking after a while. It was probably written in Jessica's notes somewhere:

Family refuses to take resident out.

Reason unknown.

Even to me.

We told Jessica about Cyril on his last visit. He was right, she understood straight away. I could see the news travel through her eyes. She'd known death before, of course – our parents, other residents she had made friends with, even one or two staff. Cyril was different, though. There was a special bond between them, and I was very worried she'd become hysterical.

She didn't. She didn't even cry. She just listened until we'd finished telling her, and then she reached over and put her hand on Cyril's arm.

'Sorry,' she said.

It was a long time before he answered. When he finally did, he said, 'Well, perhaps Margaret will take you out somewhere when it's just the two of you. The cinema, perhaps. Or the theatre.'

He turned to me and smiled, and I couldn't help but smile back. Cyril could never resist having the last word.

Two weeks later, Cyril died.

It's strange, because no matter how much time you have, you always want to barter with God for just a little more. Even the few seconds it takes to tell someone you love them. There is always something else to say, isn't there? But the clock which began ticking the day Cyril was born had finally stopped, and there would be no more I love yous, no more goodbyes. No more last words.

The people at the hospice were very kind. It takes a special sort of person to deal with dying every day, I think. I couldn't do it. I said as much to one of the nurses when I went to collect Cyril's things. Irish, she was. Dark hair, very pale. Full of smiling.

'Margaret,' she told me, 'I just think of it as helping someone on their journey. Like John Lennon.'

'John Lennon?'

'He said death was like getting out of one car and into another. Isn't that a beautiful way to look at it?'

I stared down at my carrier bag filled with Cyril's things. A cardigan, an old pair of pyjamas, a novel he never got around to finishing. His spectacles. 'It really is,' I said.

It was the first time it happened. On the journey home from the hospice. I know for a fact, because I remember sitting on the tube and holding onto that carrier bag for dear life.

It must have been a while before my change, because I was studying people's feet and trying to keep my eyes open. King's Cross, perhaps. Or the Barbican. I'd been watching a pair of alarmingly weather-inappropriate pink sandals, and I'd moved down the line of passengers to a high pair of stiletto boots. It was only then I spotted them.

Between the boots and a scruffy pair of trainers. Old brown lace-ups. Exactly the same as Cyril's. It was understandable, I suppose. People are bound to have the same footwear, but it was a few minutes before I could steel myself and see who they belonged to.

I gripped onto the carrier bag.

Because when I looked up, I realized who was wearing them.

It was Cyril.

He smiled at me across the aisle.

My mouth moved, but the only thing that came out was a small series of gasps. The woman next to me looked up from her paperback and frowned. We went through at least four stations and the only thing I could do was stare. The woman and her paperback got off at Blackfriars, and Cyril moved down the carriage and sat next to me.

'We buried you last Thursday,' I whispered. 'You're dead.'

'I am,' he whispered back and he laughed. I noticed he didn't cough afterwards any more.

'Am I hallucinating?' I said. 'Have I lost my marbles?'

He laughed again. 'No, Margaret. You haven't lost your marbles.'

'Then what in the name of God is a dead person doing riding the underground?' I tried to keep my voice lowered, but it was a battle.

'Oh, it's not just me.' He waved to a young woman who was reading the *Evening Standard* at the far end of the carriage. She gave a little wave back over the top of her newspaper.

'What?'

'It's where you go when you die,' he said. 'The underground. It's the perfect opportunity to reflect. To think about what comes next. To wait for God to make a decision about why you're there, I suppose.'

'Can everyone else see you?' I said.

'Of course they can!'

I glanced around the carriage. Men, women, old, young. A tangle of people and newspapers and carrier bags. 'How do you know who's dead and who's alive?'

'You don't,' he said.

'So why isn't the place swarming with newspaper reporters? Why has no one mentioned this before?'

'Margaret.' He turned to me. 'When does anyone ever look? We're all too busy with our own journeys to notice anyone else's.'

The train pulled into Gloucester Road.

'This is my stop!' Cyril got to his feet. He edged his way

past a teenager with a giant rucksack. 'Excuse me, young man!'

'Sorry, mate!' The lad lifted the rucksack out of the way and Cyril was gone.

I watched him walk down the platform as we pulled away.

My eyes were on stalks.

The following day, I was on the underground the minute the station opened. I studied everyone. Each face. I searched for Cyril everywhere, but I couldn't spot him. I saw several people I knew, though. My mother's cousin, who had an unfortunate encounter with a combine harvester in the mid-eighties, my old maths teacher, quite a few past members of the WI and a next-door neighbour who died in a house fire in 1972. She waved to me from the far end of the platform at Tower Hill. Not a mark on her. I'd all but given up on Cyril, when I caught up with him eastbound, eating a tuna and sweetcorn sandwich.

'You took some finding,' I said. 'Are you always on the Circle line? I still don't know how it works.'

'More often than not, and it isn't something you need worry about, Margaret. It's amazing who you find, though, isn't it? People just never bother looking.'

I studied the other people in the carriage. A few of them were asleep or staring at the floor. Most of them were absorbed by their telephone screens.

'Amazing,' I said.

We easily slipped into our old conversations and it was only as we passed through Hammersmith that I looked up.

'How's Jessica?' Cyril said.

'She misses you.' I turned to him. 'We both do.'

He reached for my hand. 'Have you taken her out?'

'You can't resist, can you?'

'I just don't understand why not,' he said.

The right words wouldn't join together. 'No,' I said. 'Nor do I.'

I started spending every day on the Circle line. You never know who you might bump into, and it's much more entertaining than the television. I keep hoping I'll spot my parents. No luck yet, but it can only be a matter of time.

Cyril is never very hard to locate, because he's such a creature of habit. We usually spend a good hour or so, passing the time of day. I keep him up to speed with the news. He never fails to ask about Jessica and he always wants to know if I've taken her out.

'I wish you'd stop nagging,' I said, only this afternoon. We were westbound, just leaving Victoria.

'It would do you both the power of good. You're sisters, after all.'

'Well that's just it, isn't it?' The words finally joined together and began spilling from my mouth. 'Sisters. Sisters go shopping together. Have lunch. Go to the theatre. They have fun. They enjoy each other's company.'

'You can do all of those things,' he said.

'Yes, but not in the same way. NOT IN THE SAME WAY!' I knew my voice was raised, because a few people looked across. 'And I'd rather have nothing than a faint, washed-out example, to remind me of something I'll never have the chance to experience.'

He stared at me.

I could feel the breath in my lungs, fighting for a way out amongst all the words. 'There. I've said it.'

'Margaret—'

'Don't even bother,' I said.

He didn't speak for a very long time. When he did, it was almost a whisper. 'Haven't you learned anything from these encounters?'

I didn't take my eyes off the advertisements on the wall. 'I don't know what you mean.'

'Whose journey are you thinking of, Margaret?'

I looked at him, but I didn't answer.

He squeezed my hand. 'Who else is in that carriage with you?'

The train stopped, and this time, we both got out. We walked along the platform in silence, through the tiled tunnelways and secret paths that take you on the next leg of wherever you might be travelling to. The only thing I could hear was the sound of our footsteps.

'I hear there's a new play opening on the South Bank,' I said very quietly, just above the footsteps.

'Yes, yes. I hear that too,' Cyril said.

We reached the escalators. 'Jessica loves the theatre, you know.'

He put his arm around my shoulder and gave me a little hug. 'I'm aware of that,' he said.

'Will I see you tomorrow?'

He leaned in and kissed my cheek. 'I'm never far away, Margaret. You've just got to keep your eyes peeled.'

He took the next stair and began travelling upwards. 'Of course,' he turned back to me. 'You know what it is, don't you?'

'What?' I could feel my eyes start to fill and I wasn't even sure why.

'Next week. You know what play is opening?'

I shook my head.

He pointed to the little adverts that hang on the wall and change every few seconds. He was moving further away.

'It's *Macbeth*!' he shouted.

I couldn't help but smile, even though the tears were running down my face.

'*Macbeth*!' He pointed again and a few people turned to look.

I could still hear him laughing as he reached the top of the escalator and disappeared into the crowds at King's Cross.

PICCADILLY

The Piccadilly Predicament

Lionel Shriver

Two 1, 2, 3 & 4s had come and gone, but this Heathrow 1, 2, 3 & 5 was the first for over twenty minutes, which more than used up the tiny leeway that Tanya Tavistock had designed into her schedule. The windows of the train approaching were black with passengers. As ever, a gap in service intensified the urgency with which everyone else with destinations to reach in a timely fashion – meaning, everyone – absolutely had to get onto this train, while greatly diminishing the possibility of doing so. What had been a promisingly under-populated segment of track on the westbound platform of Green Park was now just as chocka as every other.

Naturally, nobody got out. Using her nacreous-pink four-wheeled hard-shell as a battering ram, Tanya inserted the case in the very middle of the open double doors, and pressed as hard as 136 pounds could bring to bear – the while maintaining a Perfectly Pleasant Person Reduced Through

No Fault of Her Own to Unspeakable Rudeness expression
on her face and murmuring, 'Sorry! Sorry!' an octave higher
than her normal speaking voice, the better to make herself
sound harmlessly female – not that London tube riders cut
you any slack for being a girl. But Tanya was of the view
that passengers with planes to catch were structurally entitled.

The scrum was so tight that the rubber seals would have
pressed a pleat in her coat. The division the doors drew was
absolute. You were on the train or you were not. She shot
a side glance at the woeful left-behinds who either lacked
Darwinian drive or credulously swallowed the assurances
on the Tannoy that another 1, 2, 3 & 5 train was right
behind this one. The men abandoned on that platform were
the weak, defeatist kind that mothers warned their daughters not to marry.

Oh, God, not that Tanya had any appetite for thinking
about her mother.

The hard-shell was sufficiently planted into the crowd as
to provide an anchor, and she gripped the handle to keep
herself from falling from the carriage when the doors opened
at Hyde Park Corner. The bag was weighted down with the
profusion of second-rate presents that substituted for a single
first-rate one, abundantly food – macadamias, jars of
Harrods caviar, the thick-cut Seville marmalade any older
British couple must have missed once transplanted to Fort

Lauderdale (although if so, they surely could have ordered it online). Added up, the prices of those many small, inadequate gestures for her parents' fiftieth wedding anniversary actually came to more money than one big, brilliant gift would have cost, but the plethora had saved on thought.

Once the carriage finally disgorged more passengers than it absorbed at Earl's Court, Tanya seized a seat. She kept her roller bag clutched between her knees. Luggage stashed conventionally by the doors might tempt an opportunist on the platform to snatch it. Rocking up to this depressing excuse for a celebration in Florida with a bunch of crap still beat showing up empty-handed.

As they shambled towards Hammersmith at the pace of a toddler with a toy wagon, nearly all the other passengers were – shockers – hunched over their phones. Obviously Tanya had a mobile as well, though she was hardly tempted to check for still more texts from her sister dithering over the anniversary menu; at this point, their mother didn't know the difference between a dinner roll and a Nerf ball. Yet at forty-seven, Tanya was old enough to remember the days when people no more travelled the tube with phones than they would have with fridge-freezers. Had she watched a video of this carriage in 1990, she'd have assumed it was a science fiction film: rows of Londoners, every one of them mesmerized by a slender, transfixing rectangle. In the brave new world of the film, the residents of this city would seem to have been subjugated – stupefied into pliant zombies by a maleficent bauble.

More annoying than the dystopian panorama was the aura of self-importance that each user generated like a pulsating force field. For all the self-congratulation they exuded, you'd have thought they'd invented the bloody smart phone, as if Steve Jobs had cloned himself into infinitely receding copies before he died. They all seemed fatuously to advertise that *real other people* were actually in communication with *their own special selves*. But what was most of this lot doing really? Playing some hopped-up modern version of noughts and crosses, viewing videos of monkeys on bicycles, and watching porn.

It was on the long trundle to Acton Town that Tanya noticed the rucksack.

Large and bulging, it looked new. It sat upright, balanced against the door between carriages in the exact middle, as if carefully arranged there. The backpack was all by itself, with neither other bags nor strap-hangers anywhere near. While the seams of its main compartment were straining, the smaller exterior pockets sagged; they were empty. In contrast to the dingy rubberized flooring, grey with gungy pink bits like compacted rubbish, the nylon glared, the rattling red of hazard signage.

Alas, not only mobiles had come along since 1990, when Tanya was in her second year of uni at LSE. Back then, she wouldn't have looked at that rucksack twice.

Whenever Tanya did place her bag by the doors the way you were supposed to, she kept a fierce eye on it. Yet as she scanned the thinned-out passengers at this end of the carriage, not a single glance shot in the rucksack's direction – not even when the train rolled into Acton Town and the doors sat invitingly open. The bloke with an Eastern European pallor and a mis-buttoned overcoat had started to snore, and his own case was at his feet. The svelte Asian executive type trussed in one of those suits that looked to have shrunk in the wash was still huddled intently over his phone, as if the fate of the world rested on his *Super Samurai Rampage* score. A portly mother in full West African regalia alternated between paging a colour-coded textbook full of graphs and feeding her vacant-eyed boy congealed-looking chips. Try as she might, Tanya couldn't identify a single passenger as the plausible owner of an overstuffed rucksack.

Her older sister JJ always tried to cast her younger sibling as the anxious one – the hanky-twister terrified of risk and always convinced the sky was falling, which conveniently cast the elder sibling as confident and courageous in comparison. JJ had even 'confided' that the real reason Tanya's relationship broke up nine years ago was that Geoff had found living with her ceaseless what-ifs and 'catastrophic thinking' simply too 'exhausting'. Supposedly Geoff himself had despaired to her sister that his ex-in-waiting's permanent state of 'apprehension' was 'joyless' and 'destructive of his ability to revel in the present tense'. Thanks, JJ. Thanks for *sharing*.

But Tanya wasn't exceptionally anxious. She was thorough. She sensibly watched her back and tried to cover for contingencies, which had stood her in good stead at an advertising firm trying to navigate a radically transforming media landscape. If she had an imagination, creativity in this industry was a plus as well. Besides, to be wary of an abandoned rucksack on the tube, you didn't need an imagination. You just had to watch the news.

That's how the memory came to her, too: like a filler clip in a package on BBC 24. It would have been at Baron's Court. He was tall and lanky, possibly Pakistani, with a worn black-and-white keffiyeh around his neck and covering part of his chin. Incongruously, he'd been wearing a New York Mets baseball cap and blazing particoloured Nikes whose likely cost seemed at odds with his grubbier gear. What triggered the recollection was his manner – now *that*, my dear JJ, was what 'anxiety' looked like. His limbs were rigid, his movements jagged, as if seen under strobe. When he darted out the door – that was the word, *darted* – it had seemed a tad curious, because – well, all right, this was the part about which she was not at all sure – maybe she simply hadn't noticed him before – but she had the distinct impression that he'd just got on.

Yes, yes, yes, of *course* very few Muslims were terrorists, but a whole lot of terrorists were Muslim. Surely having put that together didn't make you a bigot.

IF YOU SEE SOMETHING, SAY SOMETHING chided overhead beside an advert for tax-filing software. Clearly, the prudent thing for a responsible citizen to do in this circumstance was to ask the carriage at large if any of them owned the rucksack.

Uh-huh. Right. Except that even if Tanya wasn't a bigot, she *was* English. Presumably she would peep, 'Sorry?' with that fluting inflection she'd developed for ramming other people's knees with a glossy pink assault weapon. It was not a voice for calling a group to order that didn't even acknowledge itself as a collective. They wouldn't pay any attention unless she aggressively made a scene.

At which point they'd all turn to her – most of them, to the eye, not born here but to a man and woman resident in this country long enough (i.e. longer than five minutes) to know that one never talked to strangers on the tube *at all*, much less did one ever address a carriage 'at large'. She would cast herself as an alarmist kook, the girly worry-wart

JJ had always claimed, and the worst kind of kook at that: one who was threatening to impede their journey, if not to instigate a colossal nightmare in which they could all be ensnared for hours. She might even offend the Asian and Middle-Eastern passengers within earshot; you never knew what provoked umbrage these days. So the prospect of this apocryphal 'Sorry?' struck her as not only preposterous, but as physically impossible. She actually went through the motions of licking her lips, clearing her throat, and opening her mouth, but nothing came out.

Besides, what would happen if she asked the carriage 'at large' and no one did claim the rucksack? She'd be obliged to ring 999. The train would be brought to a halt, at an actual station only if they were lucky. Should they be evacuated in the middle of a tunnel, she would ruin these new kitten heels with reeking greasy puddles and bash up her hard-shell on girders she couldn't see – and that was assuming the police even allowed you to take your luggage. And Tanya had a terror of rats.

The length of the Piccadilly line would slam to a halt, if not the whole underground. Convinced that just as in the vast majority of similar instances this was a false alarm, everyone on this train would hate her – as hundreds of thousands if not millions of other people throughout the system would also hate her, should they realize that Tanya

Tavistock was to blame for their cold, burnt dinners, budget-busting taxis, calamitously missed appointments, and prolonged stints in gridlocked traffic while taking replacement bus services. Why, the odds were indeed that the *Standard* would run a disdainful squib the next day about the havoc caused by an abandoned rucksack of dirty laundry.

She would miss her plane – as well as the connection in Atlanta. But with nothing blowing up or having ever threatened to blow up, the story – her excuse – would sound lame. She'd probably hide from her family the fact that she herself was the source of the tizzy over nothing.

Yet – would that be so terrible? This fiftieth in Florida filled her with dread. Was that really why the red rucksack beckoned so? Did it merely glow with the enticement of reprieve? On the other hand, if she got out of Florida because of forces that appeared to be beyond her control, she would still know that she had wanted to get out of Florida anyway, and she would worry that her family would somehow intuit that she had wanted to get out of it.

Why, in the very worst case, it would still be possible to rebook. On standby, she'd spend two nights at Heathrow on the floor. She'd get to Fort Lauderdale too late to participate in the more enjoyable pub crawls with her cousins, and only get in on the punishing main event.

By contrast, however . . . Suppose that those seams really

were straining from bulging bags of bolts and nails – and a pressure cooker or two, like the rucksacks at the Boston Marathon (which came readily to mind, as the train had just pulled into Boston Manor). Then the *Standard* article would blaze on the front page: 'Thanks to the civic-mindedness of a vigilant advertising executive (proudly promoted this morning), scores of tube passengers were saved from maiming or worse . . .' After the police defused the device by remote control, she'd be invited on *News at Ten*. On camera (in the cobalt dress with the comely cowl collar), she'd aver modestly that anyone else in her place would have done the same, since these days 'we can't be too careful'. The Met would identify the miscreant by viewing security camera footage, their screening abetted by our heroine's admirably vivid description of the suspect, down to the make and style of his trainers.

She would miss her plane. Given the subsequent commotion, conferral with detectives, and scheduling of media interviews, doubtless she would also miss the anniversary foofaraw in Fort Lauderdale in its entirety, but her absence would take a far back seat to her family's sheer relief that she was all right. Her parents, aunts and uncles, and cousins would gather round YouTube to watch the appearances of their freshly beatified celeb. JJ would have to stuff her amateur diagnosis of her younger sister's 'generalized anxiety disorder' right up her arse *through to the end of time.*

Nevertheless, why did it fall to Tanya Tavistock to police this train? No one else looked concerned in the slightest! Who from on high had selected her of all the people in this carriage to save the underground, and so to rescue a great metropolis from one more tourist-turnoff statistic? It was one thing to choose to be the hero, quite another to have heroism dumped on you – *surprise!* – as if accidentally popping up at an Ice Bucket Challenge for which you hadn't volunteered.

Speaking of ice, this carriage was nippy, thanks to its having plunked at the overground station of South Ealing for five solid minutes with the doors open in February (for no apparent reason and certainly with no explanation, as usual). Yet despite the chill, by arrival in Osterley, Tanya had begun to sweat. She was doubtless well on her way to ruining this peach top with unsightly yellow moons at the armpits. After unbuttoning her coat at the neck and fluffing air at her clavicle, she found a used napkin from Pret in its left pocket to pat dry the beads along her hairline. The while, she continued to shoot glances at the rucksack, which by now had assumed its own persona: taunting, defiant, coy in its retention of its secrets.

A last possibility remained. She clings to being a normal

British person on a normal tube trip who is normally reserved, and who therefore suppresses a peculiar mistrust of some stray piece of luggage, which has nothing to do with her, as silly and paranoid and none of her business, in the seemly British fashion. But in this scenario as well, her misgivings are well founded. Didn't it make sense, after all? What was this line's final westward destination? The airport. And weren't those nihilistic ne'er-do-wells childishly obsessed with blowing up anything to do with planes?

As the train drew into Hounslow East, Tanya was broadsided by a burst of uncharacteristic fury. All very well to live in a miraculous time when you could confer with your sister in Florida about dinner rolls while on a train to Heathrow. But despite all that lauded technological 'progress', the price was also living in a time of mindlessly regressive barbarism and arbitrary, blindingly pointless destruction and loss of life. What was wrong with those people? What made them so bitter? Most of all, what made them imagine that lighting up the vacant eyes of that little boy opposite with the fires of their righteousness would make them feel any less bitter? Nothing had advanced, really. Human beings were still animals and idiots. Like, big deal – nowadays, they were animals and idiots with smart phones. What was commonly employed to trigger a detonator? A mobile. There's your *progress* for you.

It wasn't *fair* for Tanya Tavistock to have been put in this position of having to decide whether to ruin all these passengers' day, and it was other people who had put her here – dumb people, hateful people, people who had no love of life who should just put themselves out of their own misery in private and jump off Waterloo Bridge or something, rather than dragging a bunch of strangers into their cult of suicide, too. Wasn't life hard enough, without having to worry about being deliberately run over by a lorry while walking the dog, or being deliberately incinerated en route to the airport? If you don't like it on this planet, get off. Depart your wretched mortal coil. Leave life to the rest of us, who have our own problems, believe it or not, without being saddled with yours.

'The next station is Hatton Cross,' the recorded announcement lilted. 'Customers for Heathrow Terminal 4 change here and wait for a train to Terminal 4.' The accent genteel, the feminine tones elaborately modulated, this was the fastidious voice one would use in an upscale restaurant to return the fish for being overcooked.

Christ, at least they had made it unharmed to Hatton Cross. Two more stops to go to Terminal 5. What *was* Hatton Cross, anyway? Never mind passengers too stupid to have got on the right Heathrow train to begin with; did anyone ever get off at Hatton Cross for Hatton Cross itself

– really, *anyone*? What was the purpose of it – other than to provide yet another meaningless way station at which to sit, again, tortured, for minutes at a go, doors open, waiting for nothing, or waiting for—

Tanya was perhaps more horrified by the prospect of being crippled or disfigured than she was by the prospect of snuffing it – since death was so much more abstract than a face like a dropped lasagne. But she was sitting close enough to the rucksack that, unless it was one of those incompetent contraptions that didn't go off or only partially exploded, the chances of fatality in her case were high. Now, that's what you call well and truly missing your plane.

She wanted to miss her plane. Desperately. She was not at all sure that marking the fact that her mother had put up with her domineering father for half a century was cause for raising a glass. Her sister was kidding herself, planning the menu; in the end, they would eat whatever Dad wanted. She resented that now they all had to fly to Florida for a family occasion, when every relative but her parents lived in the UK. Arguably, for her overbearing father to have bullied his wife into moving to the Sunshine State, when the good woman would have far preferred that they retired close to friends and family, only to have his wife turn into a robot in nappies – like some early generation AI, which could say *please* and *thank you* but never at the right junctures

– made for an ideal revenge. But as ever, their mother had paid the price, even for her husband's comeuppance.

The stroke (massive) was three years ago – long enough for the family to get used to it, but also long enough to establish that despite months of physical and cognitive therapy, their mother was not going to get any better. What you saw was what you got. She was wheelchair-bound and puffy, the straps of her shoes cutting into ankles tight with oedema. She smiled with half her mouth, robbing the expression of warmth; she couldn't help it, but welcoming her daughters back she looked sarcastic. She could talk, sort of, but spoke in vague formal niceties: 'Fine, and how are *you*?' Muriel Tavistock had been a vigorous woman, with a sly sense of humour behind her husband's back that functioned mostly at his expense. She'd made her own marmalade most of her life – the best in the village. As a mum, she'd recognized from the off that her children were people, with their own desires which, however odd or trivial-seeming, were worthy of respect. While woefully poor at defending her own interests, Muriel had been a terrier in the defence of her daughters', and had shielded her children from the harsher aspects of *Life With Father*. Yet each time Tanya had visited Fort Lauderdale since the stroke, the image of this lolling, oppressively polite imposter once again overwrote the memory of her real mother – the way you biro over a number with several lines to correct an arithmetic error in a cheque register, until all you can see is a three and not a five.

Five. The woman dissatisfied with her fish announced at last, 'The next station is Heathrow Terminal 5.' Although if Tanya were a terrorist, she might have targeted the previous stop – three terminals for the price of one, more bang for your buck – BA's proprietary hub was vaulting, architecturally venerated, and irresistibly spanking new . . . British Airways itself may have been privatized, but was still the UK's flag carrier, retaining an aura of the nationally iconic . . . Why, it was baldly obvious that Terminal 5 was the perfect target! As the orange digital readout advised, 'Please remember to keep all your personal belongings with you at all times', she envisaged how swiftly she would bolt for the exit, hefting the hard-shell in a fluid airborne arc behind her, the very moment the rubber lips parted. She might not have wanted to fly to Florida, but she hardly wished to die to make that point, like some idiot animal.

Yet jumping the gun somewhat, she leapt to her feet a second or two shy of the train's coming to a complete halt. In the judder of braking, she lost her balance, stumbling over the case she'd been clutching between her knees, and ending in a painful pratfall on the floor. As she glanced up, the red rucksack filled her whole field of vision, gleaming with malice.

'Please, can I help you?' The accent was posh, the hand extended brown. It was the slim Asian in the trendy suit and hip narrow tie. She accepted the lift to a stand, smoothing her skirt in embarrassment.

He looked like one of those bankers in the City, likely to travel with matching leather luggage that stacked, with a convenient exterior sleeve for a laptop. Yet in a motion both graceful and effortless – either he was stronger than he looked or the bag weighed less than it appeared to – he slung one strap of the red rucksack over a shoulder.

He insisted on righting her roll-on and lifting it briskly to the platform. 'I have to say,' he admitted, for once they were off the train the no-talking-to-strangers protocol relaxed somewhat, 'you looked so twitchy and stressed for the whole of that journey – all the brow-mopping and that – I was beginning to worry if that bag of yours contained something more frightening than clean knickers.'

'I was only nervous about missing my flight. Besides, you'd worry about *me*?' she asked, gesturing to her slight figure – nattily clad, considering that most people now took airplanes in their pyjamas, and more to the point, white.

'Women and converts,' he said lightly as they walked together towards the escalator. 'Ruthless. They're the worst.'

NORTHERN

Kat Gordon

G race was late leaving the theatre that day. They were only putting on matinees now, to contend with the blackouts, but half past three had rolled around and still the last two tickets remained unclaimed at the box office. She procrastinated by filing away the tickets for the following day, studiously ignoring the suggestion from Henry the barman that she was just waiting for an invitation back to his place. If not for him the foyer was quiet, the rolling cadences of Shakespeare and various coughs and rustles from the audience muffled by two sets of brown doors and a thick green carpet.

And then, suddenly, they were there, breathless and apologetic, and obviously from out of town.

'Can we still go in?' the woman asked. She was wearing a shabby blue coat that clashed with her purple lipstick. She was pretty, but too thin, Grace thought. We're all thin now, though.

She smiled at them, ignoring Henry's rolled eyes. 'Of course you can. Go through those doors there, and up the staircase. At the top, tap twice, and Pam – the usher – can show you to your seats.'

'*Thank* you.'

They hurried off and Grace gathered up her coat and bag, locked up her booth and came out into the foyer, pocketing the key. Out there she hesitated, savouring the last of the Vaudeville's warmth.

'How about it, then?' Henry said. 'I've never been with a redhead before. Or a Scot.' He'd sidled up to her, and now he leaned in as if to do something to her hair – smell it? Kiss it? She jumped away, disgusted.

'Not if you were the last man on Earth,' she said, and pushed her way through the double doors. The Strand in October was cold and grey, a slate-coloured grey that started at pavement level and climbed the buildings until it reached the sky. She buried her hands in her pockets. At least it wouldn't be getting dark for another couple of hours. And autumn always smelled good, even in the city. She took a deep breath. There was a smoky sweetness to the air – someone was burning leaves nearby – and an unusual smell of coffee and turpentine. The smell was coming from a young, broad-shouldered man wearing a patched up brown suit; he was barrelling down the street towards her despite a limp in his left leg. He wasn't looking up, and she didn't move quickly enough and he bumped into her. They both apologized, but he didn't raise his eyes from his feet, and barely stopped walking. Another way London was different to home.

She turned and made her way up through Covent Garden, stopping to look in shop windows. It was her mother's birthday soon, she should think about what to get her. It had to be something she could post easily – there was no money left for the train back until Christmas at the very earliest. Even then, she wasn't sure she wanted to go. She missed her parents, but she was painfully aware that her threadbare dresses were the same ones she'd arrived with almost two years ago now.

'Gracie's going to London to earn her fortune,' her father had told the neighbours when she left. 'What are you going to be, Gracie? A singer? An actress?'

'She'll be a dancer, with those legs,' one of the neighbours had said.

'Aye – I remember her doing high kicks on the garden wall no' that many years ago.'

'What about running a department store?' That from Mrs Muirfield. 'Then you could send us all some fancy new kitchenware.'

At least she was living in a nice area. Hampstead Heath

was on her doorstep, and the landlady was very protective of her young female lodger. They even had a garden with apple and pear trees and in the summer they made apple pies and compote and— No, she corrected herself. They'd *had* a garden with apple and pear trees. Last week, as they'd sat in the Anderson shelter, there'd been a deafening explosion and then a soft pattering. When they'd managed to wrench the door open, they'd seen a small crater where the lawn had been. They were all unscathed, thank God, her, and Mrs Patterson and Bert, the other lodger, who Mrs Patterson suspected of being a communist. But Grace didn't like to look out of her bedroom window now. Not down onto that gaping hole.

It was so different already, to those first few raids. It hadn't been exciting, exactly, but there was a sense of togetherness. They'd usually been in their dressing gowns, and after the all-clear was sounded Mrs Patterson would make them a cup of tea, and they'd sit around the kitchen table and talk intimately in a way they never would have before. These days Grace was often tempted just to stay in her room, with something stronger than Mrs Patterson's tea to hand.

It was the bloody *noise*. The relentlessness. It wore you down.

She realized, with a start, that people were forming a

queue at Leicester Square station ahead of her. The sky had slipped from grey to indigo almost without warning, and she was suddenly afraid. The air seemed clearer in the darkness, clear as glass, with every brick on the surrounding buildings, every window, defined. Perfect conditions for *them*.

She hurried past the queue. They weren't passengers, she knew. People were sleeping in the underground now. One of the actors last week had said there were nearly 200,000 people down there every night.

She was almost at the entrance. Two white-haired underground officials stood either side and as she reached them the one on the left nodded, and the queue slowly started to make its way through the gate.

'Are the trains still running?' she asked him.

'Till ten thirty, Miss. White lines show where the walkway for passengers is.'

He waved her through and she slipped past the people already inside and onto the escalator, realizing as she did that the man in the brown suit from earlier was directly ahead of her. From behind, she could see that his hair was longer than usual, almost shoulder length, and a deep, glossy blue-black. She wondered who he was, what he did. Where was he born? Did he go home every Sunday for a roast (not likely these days)? Funny, she thought, how you could spend half an hour on a train with someone and never see them again.

The train was busier than her usual one and she was forced to stand, holding onto one of the straps that dangled from the roof of the carriage. The windows had blackout material taped over them – for when the train surfaced at Golders Green – and directly opposite her was an advert for Brooklax Chocolate Laxative. There was only so long she could study that, so Grace took note of her fellow passengers instead. Three away from her was the brown suit again, and next to him were two older gentlemen wearing what Grace's mother would have called 'The Full Get-Up': dinner jackets, top hats and cashmere scarves. They had obviously just come from a concert and one of them was complaining loudly about it to the other.

'You can't possibly tell me that anyone prefers that atonal rubbish to Mahler?'

The other man waved his hand. 'No one goes for the music nowadays. It's a chance for some grub, that's all.'

'The programme *specifically* lists Mahler.' The first gentleman waved a piece of paper around and knocked the glasses off the woman standing next to him. 'I do apologize, Madam.'

The woman glared at him then burst into a hacking

cough. Both gentlemen recoiled, and the man in brown looked up for a moment, then quickly lost interest. Grace stifled a smile and gripped her strap tightly as the train lurched around a bend.

At Hampstead, the doors slid open much like the curtain at the theatre, revealing a densely populated stage lit by a bluish light. Grace stepped gingerly off the train, noticing that the Mahler enthusiast and his friend, and Mr Brown all followed her. She looked ahead, rather than at the scores of people sitting on the platform floor. No, she thought. Hundreds. She wondered if they had no shelters at home, or if it was simply that they had no homes any more. Out of the corner of her eye she saw two small children playing together, throwing a ball against the wall and catching it on the rebound, and something stuck in her throat.

As the queue of exiting passengers neared the end of the platform, everyone stopped suddenly, and an instinctive hush fell as they all listened out. Then they heard it – a muffled whine and cough followed by drumming and that unmistakable thud. Grace hesitated, half-turned, and came face to face with a station official.

'I wouldn't go up there, Miss. It sounds close.'

'But we've got an Anderson shelter.'

'Not worth the risk.' He looked beyond her, at all the

other passengers trying to get his attention. 'Hopefully they'll get bored soon, or the anti-aircraft guns'll get 'em, and then you can go home.'

'But is it safe here?'

He patted her arm reassuringly. 'Deepest station in the whole underground system, Hampstead. We're more than a hundred and ninety feet below ground.'

'What if they don't stop soon?'

'You can sleep down here. It's not too bad. Bit nippy, but plenty of bodies to keep you warm.'

'But I'm not – I don't have anything—' Grace felt her cheeks heating up. Don't say you don't have your dressing gown on you, she told herself.

The official moved off.

'He's right,' someone said to her left.

She looked down at a chubby, blonde girl around her own age who was inspecting her nails. The girl sighed, dropped her hands and looked up. 'There are plenty of bodies. And mosquitoes.'

'Mosquitoes?'

'Yep. They must be drawn to the smell or something.'

The Mahler gentleman had buttonholed the official now and was waving his programme around again. A few paces behind him, Mr Brown skulked, seemingly indifferent to his surroundings. Grace found, suddenly, that she wanted more than anything to see his face properly, have him meet her eye. She shook herself mentally.

'Where do people sleep?' she asked the girl.

The girl made a sweeping gesture with her arm. 'On the platform.'

'On the floor?'

'On the floor. There's talk of getting bunk beds in. Some of the other stations have them already, apparently.'

'What about . . . toilet facilities?'

'Got some buckets in the lift shaft.'

Grace felt sick and closed her eyes for a moment.

'No, really. It's disgraceful,' she heard the Mahler gentleman say. 'Haven't you heard of tuberculosis? Meningitis? Influenza?'

She opened her eyes again in time to see the blonde girl roll hers in Mahler's general direction.

Grace looked over her shoulder, wondering why. He seemed benevolent enough, if a little agitated. He had a neat black beard and very round glasses. His fist was still bunched around the programme. His friend was greying around the temples, clean shaven, and looked mildly amused.

The official had moved away again. Grace hadn't heard his response, and now she came to think of it, she couldn't hear many voices. Everyone seemed to be sitting in silence, or muttering to their neighbour. Even the children were playing quietly. There was a thickness to the air that came from a hundred or more drawn breaths.

'Come on,' the blonde girl said. 'You can share my coat.' She shuffled over, and the woman knitting on her other side moved as well without once adjusting her rhythm or looking up.

Grace sat down.

'Thank you.'

'Don't mention it.'

They grinned at each other.

'I'm—' Grace started, but the other girl cut her off.

'I don't like knowing names,' she said. 'Makes it harder if I have to read in the paper about you getting blown up.'

'I don't think I'd warrant a special naming in the paper,' Grace said. She leaned back against the tiled wall.

'Not like those two?'

Mahler and his friend were picking their way towards Grace and her companion. Mr Brown seemed to be following them almost automatically.

'Do you ladies mind if we stand here?' Mahler's friend asked.

The blonde girl rolled her eyes again.

'Not at all,' Grace said.

'Bit crowded, isn't it?'

'It's a public health liability,' Mahler said fretfully.

His friend met Grace's eye and winked. She smiled back at him.

'Well, we're all in this together now, aren't we?' he said.

'Are we?' the blonde girl said. 'Just got back from the factory, have you? Been busy helping the war effort?'

Mahler looked affronted. 'I'm sure you know we've been doing no such thing.'

She snorted. 'At least you're honest about it.'

The friend smiled again. 'What my colleague means is there are other ways of helping the war effort.'

'Let me guess – politicians.'

He made a half-bow. 'Almost right. Civil servants, I'm afraid.'

'How interesting,' Grace said, embarrassed by the other girl's bluntness.

'Do you think so?'

Her father's phrase sprang to mind. 'Well – civil servants are the grease for the political wheel, aren't they?'

Mahler raised his eyebrow and his friend laughed. 'Is that your opinion?'

If he hadn't been smiling, Grace would have thought he was mocking her. 'My dad works for the post office,' she said. 'And a cousin of mine – her husband was high up in the railways.'

'Very interesting,' Mahler said. 'You don't happen to know if he—'

'He moved to Kenya with my cousin and their children,' Grace said quickly. 'Years ago. He died out there.'

No one in the family talked about Jessie any more. Or her children. How old had Theo and Maud been when she saw them last? Probably only a little older than the children playing with their ball down here. And she'd been even younger. Only five, maybe. She'd loved Maud, she remembered—

'Oh well,' Mahler said. 'No harm in trying.'

'Is it true the government's got a shelter in the old Down Street tube?' the blonde girl asked. 'With offices and living quarters and the works?'

'I don't know where you came across that information,' Mahler snapped.

'So they do?'

'Don't you think it's important to keep the government safe?' his friend asked.

'I didn't say it wasn't. Do *you* think their lives are worth more?'

He took out a cigarette case, chose a cigarette and lit it. 'I'm afraid I don't follow.'

'They were talking about building deep shelters in Finsbury,' the blonde girl said. 'In the garden squares. But they didn't. They won't – Finsbury's a working-class borough.'

'Ah—' He blew out smoke. 'A communist in our midst.'

'So what if I am?'

'Don't you think the government takes its responsibilities seriously? They're trying to run the country for everyone. Who's going to do that if they're all blown up?'

'What's the point in a government if all the citizens are dead?'

'*Touché*,' he murmured, and turned to look directly at Grace instead. 'What do you think, my dear?'

Mr Brown looked up and met her gaze then. His eyes were green. For some reason she'd thought they'd be brown.

'I don't—'

He dropped them again.

'I've put you on the spot,' Mahler's friend said.

Mahler cleared his throat loudly. 'Must you smoke that down here?'

His friend dropped the cigarette without a word and ground it under his heel.

He was so solid, Mr Brown. She stole a look at his hands; they were huge, but delicate at the same time, long fingers, neat. Pianist's hands, she thought, without knowing why.

The blonde girl squeezed Grace's arm. 'Are you OK?' she asked, sounding concerned.

'I'm fine.' Grace smiled weakly at her.

'Are you sure?'

She lowered her voice. 'Where did you say the facilities are?'

'In the lift shafts. They close the two on the left.'

Grace stood, avoiding looking at the others, and made her way in the direction indicated, picking her way over more people slumped against walls and lining the stairs.

A middle-aged woman was leaning against the wall next to the lifts.

'Go on in,' she said. 'This one's empty.'

'Thank you,' Grace murmured.

It was even colder in there, and smelled strongly of urine. A single lantern placed on the floor lit up the enamel bucket. Grace lifted her face. The ceiling seemed miles away; she could only tell where it was because there was another lantern up there, its light shining through the space between the lift and walls. Must be so anyone who still needs shelter can find their way, she thought, and wondered if a station official was up there with it, ready to guide the seeker into safety.

She lowered her gaze again and made her way to the centre of the floor, suppressing a shudder, then lifted her skirt, rolled her underwear down to just below her knees and squatted over the bucket. At first nothing came. Grace tried to relax, and eventually a long stream came gushing out. She'd wondered if people sitting outside would hear. But no, it was covered by the whistling of the wind around her, and then, without warning, the *rat-a-tat-tat* of the anti-aircraft guns sounded, echoing loudly in the empty, metal space.

She jumped, felt a splash of liquid hit her shoe. Above her, the clamour continued. She forced herself to hurry, shaking herself over the bucket to get rid of any remaining drops, then pulling her knickers and stockings back up and running out of the shaft, out of earshot of whatever was going on above her.

She collided with Mr Brown for the second time that day and slipped. He caught her, one hand on her elbow and one arm round her waist. She let out a yelp and grabbed at his lapel, hauling herself upright again.

'Sorry,' he said.

His voice was low, but clear, too. He was so close she could see the small white scar on the bridge of his nose. She wondered where it came from, if it was the same incident that had injured his leg.

'It's my fault,' she said. 'I was running – I didn't feel safe when the guns started . . . Silly of me.'

'I don't blame you. They're awful loud in there,' the woman standing next to the lifts said, and Grace suddenly remembered they weren't alone. 'Scares me half to death every time I hear them. But we're safe down here, love.'

'The station official said.'

'He's right. Thank God they started letting us in – they had orders at first to shut the gates when the bombing started.'

Grace looked around at all the faces. No one else was paying them much attention. A young woman was feeding her baby, and near her a family of six were playing cards quietly. Several people were sleeping, an old man was smoking his pipe and his wife a cigarette. She looked closer and saw their free hands were interlinked. They were all just ordinary people. The idea that they could be turned away shocked her.

'*Why?*' she asked.

'They thought large shelters would incubate defeatism,' Mr Brown said. He rammed his hands into his pockets. 'The worry was that everyone would talk about how bad it was and come to the conclusion that the war wasn't worth fighting.'

'That's *awful.*'

'Oh, I'm just grateful they changed their minds,' the lift woman said. 'That's all that matters.'

'Not if people died because they couldn't get in,' someone said behind Grace.

She turned and saw that the blonde girl and Mahler and his friend had followed them.

'The government takes everything into consideration,' Mahler's friend said. 'Sometimes hard decisions are made for the good of the people.'

The blonde girl looked angry now. 'And turning people away is good for them?'

'Sometimes you have to consider elements – unstable elements.'

'Poor people? Immigrants?'

He smoothed his shirt front. 'Anyone is welcome to their own private shelter, but we don't need a case of mass hysteria in one of the communal ones.'

'Anyone vulnerable is allowed to panic,' the blonde girl said. Her cheeks were shiny with tears. 'People like you are the reason my mum's dead.'

Grace took her hand. 'I'm so sorry. A bomb?'

'No.' The blonde girl scrubbed her eye with the heel of her other palm. 'My dad killed her after he drank too much one night. I kept telling her to leave, but she had no safe place to go.'

Grace didn't understand how the two were linked, but Mr Brown seemed to. He touched the blonde girl on the arm, briefly, and nodded when she looked at him.

'Sorry,' he said.

Mahler and his friend were quiet. The woman next to the lifts was tutting. 'Poor lamb.' She stooped and picked up a Thermos standing by her feet. 'Have a sip of this.'

The blonde girl dropped Grace's hand and took the Thermos. She gulped down whatever was in it then tried to pass it back. The woman waved it away. 'You keep it, dearie.'

'Thank you.'

She looked tearful again, and Grace tried to distract her. 'Did you need to use the facilities?'

'I wanted to see how you were. You went sort of green before you left.' She jerked her thumb at Mahler and friend. 'I don't know why they followed me.'

'I wanted to see if there was a space where I wasn't at risk of contracting some god-awful disease,' Mahler said.

His friend took out his cigarette case again. 'I felt like some exercise, myself.'

'And I wanted to talk to you.'

She turned her head and looked directly at Mr Brown. 'Oh?'

'Well *this* is interesting,' the blonde girl said.

Mahler sniffed.

'I got on the train because of you,' Mr Brown said. 'I noticed you on The Strand, and then, when you were behind me on the escalator. Didn't you see me hesitate at the bottom? I was waiting to see which direction you were going in.'

'Where did you need to go?'

'Balham.'

He cocked his head, looking her in the eye. A strange surge of energy coursed through her, starting at her toes and ending up around her ears. She wondered briefly if she'd been poisoned. You heard about that sort of thing happening in wartime.

'What were you going to do?' she asked.

'Nothing.' He shrugged. 'Ride the train with you.'

'Oh?'

'You never know which bomb is the one with your name on it.' He looked away. 'I liked looking at you; I liked the way you smelled. I just wanted to have that for a little longer.'

'I see,' she said.

From above, there was a particularly loud whine, and thud, and the lights flickered, the ground trembled. Someone nearby let out a panicked cry, and grit and soot started raining down on their heads. Grace reached out and grabbed Mr Brown's hand; she felt the blonde girl reach out and hold her other hand. More people were crying or screaming now, and among the din she suddenly realized she was calling for her mother. She closed her eyes and focused inwards. Don't panic. This isn't how I die, she thought. This isn't how I die. Am I dying? No – the shaking's stopped. I can still breathe.

She opened her eyes. A cloud of dust still emanated from the lift shaft, everyone was covered in a fine layer of dirt, and a few tiles had fallen off the wall near the smoking couple, but otherwise everything was normal. Or almost normal. She noticed that everyone was holding someone's hand. Even Mahler and his friend were clasped to each other. She met his friend's eye and he looked away.

'Thank fucking Christ,' someone said loudly, and someone else laughed. Then they were all laughing, brave together. Grace was still holding Mr Brown's hand, and she squeezed it tightly.

'I don't know your name,' she said.

WATERLOO & CITY

Number Five

Joe Mungo Reed

It takes me a while to find my father at the location. The trailers and catering vans are parked up a cobbled street next to the City of London Magistrates' Court, little activity around them. It is the penultimate Sunday before Christmas, dawn. The air is misty, damp, bearing a faint smell of the river. The security man at the entrance to the lane wants to see a lanyard, which I don't have. 'I'm the director's daughter,' I say.

'You could be,' the man says and shrugs. 'And maybe I still shouldn't let you through.' I frown at him. 'People don't always feel so positive about their families,' he adds.

'Right,' I say. 'We're close, though. We're fine.'

He exhales through his nose, his breath visible in the frigid air. 'This time of year in particular,' he says.

I take out my phone and fumble to unlock it with cold fingers. A taxi passes down the road: an old one, faded to a bluish-grey, a blocky body, burning oil, leaving a visible trail of smoke. I turn back and see Kathy over the shoulder of the security man. I shout to her. She registers my presence, comes over. Kathy is the assistant to my father's assistant, Henrietta. She is carrying three phones, a litre of oat milk and a small claw hammer.

'They're down in the tube already,' Kathy says. 'They've been shooting for an hour.' She repositions her load under her arm then draws out her lanyard and waves it at the security man, who steps back to let me pass.

Down on the platform are many people of a greater category of importance. There are lots of lights and clipboards and men with cargo pockets on their trousers: the secondary drama of a shoot here in this enactment of necessity, this playing out of particular roles. The air smells of soot and metal and ancient dust. A train pulls into the station. Its doors open. My father is in the middle of a carriage. He sits on a bench seat like a passenger, slumped a little, his feet crossed beneath him, the outer edges of his lime-green running shoes resting on the floor. To his left stands a cameraman, a lighting crew, and a couple of sound people. In front of the camera are actors and extras pressed together as if part of a commuting crowd. My father dresses like a director: that is, a schlub with an expensive pair of glasses. He tends to lose weight on shoots. His face gains definition. A brief catch in his gaze suggests that he has seen me. I get onto the section of train behind my father and the camera. Here are people who I recognize, who recognize me: my father's director of photography, Alexi; the assistant director, Olaf; my father's PA, Henrietta. 'How's university?' says Henrietta.

'It's good,' I say. 'It's the start of the holidays.'

'Well, it certainly isn't here,' she says.

Ahead, my father has his eyes closed as if meditating on something.

The train moves up to speed. 'Camera?' says Olaf. The cameraman nods.

'Sound,' says my father. He opens his eyes. The camera assistant claps the sticks. 'Action,' says my father.

A man amongst the press of bodies at the other end of the carriage raises his gaze towards a point behind the cameraman's head. He is a serious actor, known as much for his work in theatre as on film. He is thin, a kind of needy skinniness to him. This close, I am struck by the oddness of his features: his wide jaw, his severe brow, the way his eyes bug out. His is a handsomeness that only resolves itself as such on the screen or stage. He says, 'Do you expect me to believe that?'

I watch my father. He is looking at the ridged floor of the underground carriage. He wiggles his head as if signalling indecision. He says, 'Cut. This is getting closer to what I'm looking for.'

My father is mildly famous for his working methods, his name associated in industry circles with struggle. He is known for being exacting, meticulous. His shoots always overrun. His tendencies in this respect have only become more pronounced in recent years, those who work with him more accepting of them. People have gained an idea, I suppose, that the ordeal of working with him attests to the seriousness of his films, the clarity of his vision.

This present film, he has told me, is about a banker who gets stalked by a street performer. The theme is economic inequality, apparently. 'It's sort of French in its preoccupations,' he said on the phone when I called him two days ago. He talks guardedly of the production, and I sense in this guardedness that he has hopes for it, aspirations towards those awards and plaudits that still elude him.

The train stops at Waterloo. The platform is empty. The doors do not open. Outside, the driver trots to the other end of the train. My father has his eyes closed. He rubs at his lids with his thumb and forefinger. We start again. We get up to speed. Another take begins. The lead actor says, 'Do you expect me to believe that?'

My father cuts in. 'Say the words,' he says, 'as if they're being said by someone else.'

When I was a child, my father was often away for months at a time. When he had returned from a shoot in Argentina that lasted nearly a year, I recall that he told me to wash my hands before dinner, and I thought, Who the fuck are you to tell me that? I was angry, and I could rage at him like I have raged at nothing since. But it was so boring feeling like that in the end.

Few stories of omission are so simple, one comes to see. My siblings and I wanted for nothing. We travelled. We met interesting people. In the summer we went to a mansion on the Mediterranean. My father would appear for short periods of the holidays, like a returning king. 'You're a fierce and jealous tribe,' he said, proudly. I remember that.

I am one of seven. Sometimes he'd go away and I'd wonder if he'd even know me when he got back, whether he'd be able to pick me out of the mass of the rest of us. I was the fifth-oldest, and I took to calling myself Number Five. I would sign letters to him 'Number Five'. 'It's Number Five,' I would say, when I reached him on the phone. He thought it was very witty, though. He continued calling me Number Five long after I had given it up myself.

We travel back and forth between the two platforms for an hour and a half, the actor repeating the line, my father cutting in to offer an abstruse direction. Sometimes they get two takes in before the train turns around, sometimes only one.

The actors look thoroughly pissed off, which, to my father's credit, suits their roles as commuters. Between takes the man holding the boom mike puts it down on the seats beside him. He hooks his thumbs in his armpits and paddles his elbows like wings. He breathes as if these movements relieve a pain.

'Coffee?' says Henrietta to the carriage. Henrietta is unique in her ability to neglect the conventions of my father's sets, to intrude on his attention without censure.

He looks up. 'Two more,' he says.

When he has tried four more takes, my father says, 'We are approaching what I'm looking for.' The train door reopens and we troop out onto the platform.

He comes over and kneads my shoulder. He smells sour, familiar: a hint of sweat, Juicy Fruit chewing gum on his breath. He is energized on days like these in a way that still surprises me. 'Laura,' he says. 'You're having fun?'

'I do love hearing the same line a hundred times,' I say.

'We're not half done,' he says. 'Don't you remember when you wanted to be a director? When you used to come on set with a straw hat like the one I used to wear?'

'I think that was another of your children,' I say.

'A little clapperboard, if I remember rightly. The name of whatever film I was working on then scrawled on it in chalk. Very cute.'

'I don't remember this,' I say. 'It was someone else, I think. I can't imagine you being particularly charmed by it.'

He chuckles in agreement. An intern arrives with coffee. 'Well, why are you here?' he says. His hands go up in pantomime confusion. He laughs again.

'I told you when I called,' I say.

'Something about your brother selling pencils?'

'Mark quit university,' I say. 'You remember this, right? He's working in an upmarket stationery shop now.'

'You are someone who arrives with an agenda. You are the practical one. When I consider this, I agree that perhaps you were not the budding director I was remembering.'

'No.'

'It's not a bad thing. Don't get me wrong.'

'It's not the fact that he's selling pencils,' I say. 'It's just that he seems unhappy. Lost. He's broken up with Claire.'

'He's what, twenty-two?'

I nod.

'Christ. At twenty-two I hadn't even been *near* a university. I'm not sure I could have tied my own shoelaces. Lost wouldn't begin to describe me at twenty-two.'

Larry comes past. Larry is American, a fixture on my father's sets, though I have no idea what his defined role actually is. He says, 'We're blowing money out of our asses on this one.' Loudly, to no one in particular. My father smiles. He is always cheered by the presence of Larry, by Larry's saying things like this.

My brother Mark and I live together in Newcastle. Mark is older, arrived in the city two years before me, dropped out of university in his final year. We share a messy flat. Like our father, Mark has blue-green eyes. He has some of the old man's grandness in him: meeting him, you might think that he is very modest, but I have come to think that his self-containment is more like an opening, a space made with an expectation that others should advance towards him. He is the kind of boy who sits on the edge of parties waiting to be noticed. He has abandoned a degree in anthropology. 'The system is irredeemable,' he told me. 'There is a limit to the insights possible within the framework.'

He works short shifts in the stationery shop, selling leather-bound notebooks, pencils in all the different grades. I have snuck in and watched him serve customers. He is effective in the way of upmarket waiters, tailors. He does the job with a controlled scorn for those who seek his assistance, powered, I sense, by a fiercer disdain for himself.

'I appreciate your concern for your brother,' my father says.

'That's a very fatherly way to phrase it.'

'Why, thank you.' He sips his coffee. 'Maybe university is not for him. The stationery shop complaint isn't good for you. People need pencils and pens. Someone needs to do that job. Don't be a snob.'

'Would you want to do it?'

He waves his hand around in the air. 'I do this,' he says.

We get back onto the train, then. My father tries another eighty minutes of takes. 'This one is more intense than the last one,' says Henrietta. 'I think he thinks this could be it.'

My father has never won an Oscar. Perhaps this will be the film to get him one: Best Picture or Best Director.

Maybe the serious theatre actor will win one and not my father. If so, he is being made to suffer for this beforehand. 'Cut,' says my father. 'You're surprised to find yourself saying the words, but it is a surface-level surprise. Another part of you understands that this interaction is fated. You have carried these words within you for a very long time. Also, remember that you have a trapped nerve in your back.'

We get off again for more coffee. 'This is the most filmed tube line in London,' my father tells me. 'Waterloo and City. Closed on Sundays, and so available for hire. Often art people rebadge it, make it the Central line, the Victoria line. I wouldn't like to do that. Our character works in the City, anyway. It's perfect as it is.'

'Only four minutes before you need to turn around, though,' I say.

'Three minutes forty, on average,' he says.

'Why not have the train driver go slower? Get more takes in?'

'Then the motion of the train is wrong. The rattle and resonance would be off.'

In another life, he could have been an ordinary father, possessor of the same shoddy knowledge as other men his age: interested in trains, in urban arcana. I sip my coffee and think I should tell this to friends of mine too admiring in the way they ask about him. 'The words,' I say. 'The words you have him saying are total shit.'

He looks at me with pleasure. 'Of course,' he says. 'This is the language people live in, think in. Junk language. Easy. Close to hand. The point is not the words. The point is what is between the words.'

'1 sec,' I say.

'I'm entering a new phase,' my father says. 'Or concluding one.'

We get back on the train. Everybody tries again. We keep going until Henrietta says, 'Is it not time for lunch?'

My father assents. 'Don't get me wrong,' he says. 'We're not quite there, but the trajectory of this shoot is good.'

We ride out of the station on an escalator. 'You're staying with your big sister Katya?' says my father.

'Yes,' I say.

'Derek?'

'Derek is OK.'

'Not our people, I always think.'

'You're coming for Christmas Day?'

'Yes,' says my father.

'Mark isn't coming down,' I say.

'Right,' says my father. *Not this again*, his expression says. 'Well. It is his choice.'

'I'm just saying call him. Check up on him.'

'You've made all this effort to come here just to tell me this?'

Henrietta is lingering by the catering vans when we arrive at street level. 'There is food in your trailer,' she says to my father. 'No more of that salad dressing you didn't like.'

'It wasn't dressing,' says my father. 'It was mayonnaise and a memory of cheese.' He waves his hand. 'I think we're going to go somewhere nearby, anyway.' He checks with me. I nod my assent.

We walk away from the shoot on quiet pavements. A ruffled pigeon hobbles out of our way, one of its feet a scarified nub. 'How's university, my young philosopher?' he says. He is wearing just a thin jersey, but seems untroubled by the cold.

'Fine,' I say.

'Give me one of your riddles.'

I do not want to give him Wittgenstein to get his fierce autodidactic teeth into. I tell him about moral luck, then: the two drunk drivers, one who encounters a child in the road and hits that child, and one who gets home without incident on empty roads.

'The point?' he says.

'They performed the same actions,' I say, 'they were equally reckless, and yet one, most people feel, is more blameworthy.'

'The one who hit the child?'

I shrug *Yes, of course.* 'We don't like to think of chance playing a part in judgements of this kind.'

'It's good,' he said. 'I like it. It proves what?'

'It disquiets us,' I say. 'It challenges our intuitions. It breaks up the narrative of character.'

'I love it,' he says. 'You are good at this. This study befits you.'

'I went to a conference,' I say. 'I met people who were really good.'

'Yes?'

'Men and women made to think,' I say. 'People who talk too fast for me, who began from assumptions I could not grasp.'

'Strange?' he says.

I nod. 'A bit.'

Really, I thought of nature documentaries I had seen about the extreme depths of the oceans, the creatures they find down there: huge-eyed fish with lanterns on their heads, tiny translucent organisms. They were wonderful and terrifying, the others there. I met a man who said, 'I study the history of retrocausality.' He wore a full tracksuit. He awaited my follow-up questions. They were young people freakishly destined to be doing what they were, resolved only on their precise pursuits.

We come to a branch of Pret A Manger. My father waves his thumb at it. This is what he has been looking for, I suppose: the staple of my last years before university. There was a branch three doors down from the house. We ate sandwiches morning, noon and night.

'Sure,' I say. We go in and the smell is so familiar, the clatter of service, the light.

'Go and save a place,' says my father. He points to the stools facing out of the window. 'Avocado and crayfish?'

'Yes.'

I go to a stool. I turn in it and watch him queuing, half listening as the cashier asks him whether he wants a bag. He looks behind him at the line. He looks out of the door. There is a young man out there, smoking, wearing a lanyard from the shoot. My father goes and taps on the glass. The man comes in, talks to my father, hands him a £20 note. My father smiles in apology.

'I forgot my wallet,' he says, when he arrives with the sandwiches on a plastic tray.

'I could have paid,' I say.

He shakes his head. 'They have expenses. There is a system.' He guts open the packaging of his sandwich. He slices his sandwich into quarters with a black plastic fork.

'Uncle Rob is coming for Christmas,' I say.

'Your sister is paying for his flights?'

This seems low, so I do not reply. Rob is my father's brother, a blues musician, recorder of more than thirty albums, recipient of ten-pence royalty cheques from Spotify. He lives in an apartment in Vilnius, a city which, according to him, is cheap, surprisingly pretty, and famous for a number of palatable delicacies made from pork.

'He's made a new album,' I say.

'That's nice,' says my father. 'I hope this one does well for him.' He chews. Outside the window is a dog tied to a lamp-post, rising onto its hind legs, falling down again. 'He's never forced it,' says my father.

'Or things have never fallen for him.'

'You have to shake things a bit for things to fall.'

'He's good at Christmas,' I say. 'Mum always liked Rob.'

'Of course. He is me without the hard edges. What is not to like.'

'So why stay hard-edged?' I say.

My father has embarked on eating the final quarter of his sandwich. He helicopters his free hand around his head as if to say *this*: the moment, the city, the film crew we have just left behind.

I know the waypoints of my father's life. I have heard him talk about them often. He is at the level of fame where half the people he meets know his name before he says it. One must have a story in these circumstances, a front to present to the world.

He left his boarding school without qualifications. He wanted to be a painter. He went to Italy, because he felt that was the thing to do. 'I had no talent, but my big brother was a musician,' he tells people, 'so I couldn't do that. I picked painting at random.' He was eating in a restaurant in Naples one lunchtime when an American couple came in, were seated next to him. 'They went on to have the most fantastic argument,' he says. 'They poured it all out, thinking no one around them understood.' He listened. 'She kept talking about the way he snorted as he laughed. He kept complaining about the expense of the cocktail she had ordered in Rome.' He loved the intimacy, the fact he could picture their lives, the way his sympathy swung back and forth. This could be a film, he thought.

He talks of this story as the official history.

'What's the unofficial?' I once asked.

'I watched a lot of great films and wrote a lot of shit scripts,' he said. 'Just like everyone else.'

We walk back to the station in light drizzle. The day is already falling towards dusk. 'Seriously,' he says. 'You worry about your brother?'

'Yes,' I say. 'Of course.'

'Is he going to do something?' he says. 'Is that what you're implying? A breakdown? Suicide?'

I wonder whether he knows he is outmatching me, if he has foreseen I can't follow him there. I lack his capacity for overstatement. 'What about conventional unhappiness?' I say.

He throws up his hands, exhales. 'Conventional unhappiness?! What do I do with that?'

We stop to cross the road. The set is there, humming with activity. People are clocking the arrival of my father already. 'I admit it,' he says, 'you've had a tough time, and perhaps I didn't help you through it as much as I could.

119

But he is older; it's those of you who were teenagers who I worry about sometimes.'

The thing he is talking around is my mother's death, four years before, but I do not want this corny, half-built regret, this ordinary fatherly admission. 'But what if it's not about that?' I say.

He looks at me. 'If it's not about that, then I don't have a clue what I am doing.'

We travel down the escalator into the station. People are in position already, waiting for him. On the platform the crowd parts to allow him onto the train. I follow in his wake.

He went off on a shoot the week after my mother's funeral. 'It's what she would have wanted,' he said, and I have never thought he was wrong. His work was both their work in the end. She had made that choice. She had been an actor when she met him. I massaged her feet a great deal when she was ill. She had strong feet: high arches. She was a good dancer. She looked younger in the first weeks of the disease, which took weight from her face, which seemed, oddly, to relax her features. I asked her then if she regretted giving up the acting. 'We had Katya and it was clear,' she said. 'I am not talking about men and women. I felt my previous life was small. I did not need it. The world did not shift for him in this way. You get into a thing like that, and the kind of person you are becomes obvious.'

He walks into the train, takes his seat in the same position he has occupied all day. I go through the other sliding door, into the back of the carriage. I stand beside Henrietta. 'Good lunch?' she says.

'Yes,' I say.

'I heard you won a prize for a philosophy essay.'

'Came second.'

'You'll do a PhD?' she asks.

'I don't know,' I say.

The train starts to move again. My father does takes for two more hours. We break for coffee. It is no doubt already fully dark outside, and I must return to my sister's house for dinner.

M y mother always said that my father's story about the restaurant in Italy was bullshit. 'He wouldn't have actually listened,' she said. 'He would have leaned over and coached each of them in what to say.'

I think that she was right, and yet I also know that my father believes his own story to be true: if not a full history of his creative beginning, at least an active part.

He has absolute trust in his own narratives, in the essentiality of his obsessions. When I was younger my parents never watched the news, never read newspapers. There was just my father's work. 'If something important happens,' my father would say, 'someone will kick down the door and shout it at us.'

But how to live and not await the sound of a boot against wood?

My father limps off the train. He is tired himself now. He drinks a coffee slowly. He studies the tiling on the wall of the station. I tell him that I must go. 'You don't want to stay until the bitter end?' he says. He laughs. He is drawing together the last of his reserves.

'I think I can bear to miss it,' I say.

He smiles. He turns back towards the train.

I know how it will go. He will keep shooting all evening. He will hold to his prerogative, that claim to hear something between those words that others do not. He will take them all to their limit. He will push until the moment must declare itself. He will say to everyone's surprise that that is it, that they are done, release them all so simply. He will believe fully in this, in the necessity of it all, in the miraculous resolution of the day in this single flawless take.

He will leave all those people clearing away the equipment from the platform. He will ascend on the escalator, to a waiting taxi. He will return to the house, the two rooms he lives in there.

How does one get that? Such control, such absorption, such faith in one's own story? The quiet house. The alarm clock set for four fifteen. No thought of life another way. How does one get that? I want to know.

CENTRAL

Worm on a Hook

Tyler Keevil

I shouted Shona's name, so it resonated across the underground station, even though my daughter was right beside me – or right behind me, really, struggling to keep pace – and it was her eagerness to catch up and my unwillingness to wait that had set up the impending accident: my parental instincts clocked her velocity, and how she was looking sideways, distracted by a pigeon pecking at some chips, and oblivious to the pillar looming before her.

All of that registered in less than a second, giving me just enough time to enunciate two syllables – *Sho-na* – which stretched agonizingly across the five feet between us, serving only to draw the attention of my wife (about a dozen steps behind, also struggling to keep pace with me) to what was about to happen when Shona's face collided with the pillar, which it did: the impact both visible and audible. Her head seemed to stop before her body, like a boxer walking into a stiff jab, and a blunt smack reverberated. It was as if I could feel it through the air molecules, through the station floor beneath my feet: a miniature earthquake that rocked me and destabilized the ground. I stumbled, caught myself, looked around – expecting other commuters and travellers to be falling over, clinging to each other, grabbing onto handrails for support.

Only they weren't. A couple of people looked with concern at the three-year-old girl who sat down clumsily, one leg folded beneath her, and a few others glanced at me as I spun to double back, cradling Samuel, our six-month old, in the carrier on my chest, awkwardly loping while trying not to disturb him. I clung to the vague, deluded hope that it would just be another scrape and bruise to add to the long list Shona had already racked up, her body unbelievably resilient, her pain threshold preternaturally high: the fall from the buggy; the tumble off the slide; the bump on the window sill: all these moments that she had faced, and endured.

But Shona wasn't screaming or crying, and that silence seemed ominous, and the severity of it was telegraphed to me by Lowri, approaching from the other side, who had a clear view of our daughter's face. 'She's cut,' Lowri said, in a tone that was too controlled, too restrained. I crouched and adjusted Samuel, twisting my neck so I could see what my wife had seen. A streak of blood leaked from an inch-long gash on Shona's cheek. The surrounding skin was already puckered, swollen, going molten. And I was thinking to myself: this is bad, this is really bad, this is not good.

It might have played out differently if we'd been in Canada, where I grew up, or Wales, where Lowri is from, and where we live. In those familiar locations we would have been more confident and assured, capable of dealing with calamity, bad luck, the unforeseen.

But we weren't in either of those places. We had come down to London, because our old friend Beatrice from Los Angeles was in town with her wife, and they couldn't make it out to Wales to see us because Bea had an intense schedule lined up, meeting with various donors for her international charity. Lowri had been inclined to skip a visit: the prospect of the long drive down, with a baby and a three-year-old, to navigate London by car, train and tube, filled her with a kind of existential dread.

I had campaigned to go. Friends from our past, particularly North American friends, rarely visited the UK. Plus it was Bea, who had meant so much to us at one time, and who carried with her a kind of benevolent glamour, moving in the circles she did, raising funds from high-profile sources: celebrities, politicians, CEOs. On top of that Lowri and I were at that stage of child-rearing where we had grown terrified that the children were not just taking over our lives, but *becoming* our lives.

And so even though it bothered me that Bea couldn't make time to visit us, I was still intent on visiting her, and proving to her and ourselves that we weren't *those* kind of parents, but another kind: the kind that could casually load cot, blankets, milk bottles, toys, picture books, nappies (what I would call diapers), baby wipes, fruit snacks, and all other manner of supplies into the back of our battered hatchback and drive five hours down the motorway, making frequent stops for bathroom breaks, for feeds, for much needed coffee, and across London during rush hour through the congestion zone – inevitably forgetting to pay – and to our Airbnb, which (as ever) wasn't in quite as good an area as we'd expected, all the while trying to maintain some semblance of civility and pretend we were having fun, calling Bea to tell her we'd arrived and couldn't wait to see her, deciding to meet her at the British Museum the next day, struggling to get the kids down and weathering another sleepless night (Shona didn't like being away, and Samuel was still teething) before getting up and walking to the nearest tube station to ride the Central line across London to Holborn (again at rush hour), at which point the absurdity of my ambitions, the sheer hubris of the endeavour, had caught up with us and I had led our three-year-old daughter into a concrete pillar.

Which is how we'd arrived where we were at.

The pillar itself was particularly wicked-looking. It had sharp-edged ornamentation: little baroque flourishes like you might see on a gothic gate or portcullis. One of those edges had split the skin of Shona's face, neat as a scalpel, just above the cheekbone. A sliver of white showed in the centre of the cut. Fatty tissue, maybe. Or the hypodermis. I'd never seen my child injured in that way: not beyond scrapes and scratches that were almost endearing in their scale, little boo-boos and owies.

This was not a boo-boo or owie.

'I didn't see it,' I said.

Lowri hadn't said anything about it being my fault, but there was a set to her jaw: the clench of suppression, the pent-up frustration, the bitter silence of implied accusation.

'The baby wipes,' I said, desperate, as if they could wipe away not just the blood but the hurt and the wound and my guilt as well.

Lowri furiously unzipped her handbag and rooted through it, discarding various bits of jetsam in the process: lipstick, make-up mirror, tampons, until she found the wipes and tugged several out, using them in a bunch to dab at the blood, while avoiding the cut itself. Blotches soaked through the tissue, blossoming like Rorschach blots. Shona was emerging from the initial shock of it, but hadn't started to cry yet. Plaintive moans faltered from her mouth like the vibrations of a throat-singer. I told her that it was OK, that she'd be OK.

'We need to get her to a hospital,' Lowri said. 'That's going to need stitches.'

I looked at her, dazed and disbelieving. 'It's not that bad.'

'It's that bad.'

'Can you look on your phone?'

I no longer had a smart phone. I had drowned mine in a canal, while canoeing on a stag party, so was temporarily stuck with an old brick: no internet or wireless or maps. Lowri told me to hold Shona and I knelt by her and took the wipes and applied pressure to the cut, trying to comfort her while simultaneously shushing Samuel who had begun to make his soft but urgent grunts that usually presaged a bout of wailing.

Lowri pulled her phone out of her open purse – the innards of which still lay sprawled about us like the contents of an emptied stomach – and tapped at it.

'What do I look for?' she asked me.

'Just look up hospital. Type in hospital or whatever.'

She tried, then stopped, raised the phone, rotated on the spot, like a diviner dowsing for water. And she of course had no signal, which any Londoner would have known – seeing as we were underground, in what amounted to a concrete bunker.

While all this went on people continued to pass to and fro in the station, moving about us in currents of legs and feet. We were between the ticket machines and barriers, an obvious obstruction. In passing people looked, and – seeing the situation – hurried on. They no doubt sensed the pain, the tension, the parental panic, and it must have seemed safest to avoid that.

'We'll have to ask somebody,' Lowri said, shoving her phone away. She scrambled across the floor, chasing errant detritus from her purse, which she refilled.

'Could you take Sam?' I asked her. 'I'll carry Shon.'

This led to the convoluted passing of the carrier and baby from me to her, unstrapping and re-strapping, wriggling and squirming, before he was settled. Then I crouched and lifted Shona, cradling her across my torso while also applying pressure to the cut. When I picked her up she started shrieking, harsh and repetitive as a fire alarm. People gave us a wider berth: this bubble of space formed around us as we staggered towards the ticket barriers, sweaty and bedraggled, like survivors of some apocalypse, searching for somebody who could help us.

We found Charlie. Charlie was tall and lean as a lodge pole and had the kind of stoop you develop from constantly having to duck. He wore an official-looking tube person uniform that vaguely resembled a cop's, except of course he had no pistol or nightstick. He saw us coming, and heard us (it was impossible not to hear us) and observed our approach with his eyebrows raised in surprise and concern.

I knew his name was Charlie because he had a nametag: *Charlie*.

'Our daughter cut her face,' I said, pointlessly. There was blood all over her shirt, all over my hand and the wipe.

'Where's the nearest hospital?' Lowri said.

It seems strange to me now that we didn't ask Charlie if there was a first aid station on site, or a trained first aider. For all I know, Charlie himself could have administered first aid. But we had it in our heads that we needed a hospital, and he accepted this.

'Yeah, man,' Charlie said laconically. 'That lass needs seeing to. Here's what you got to do, you hear me?'

'We hear you,' I assured him. 'We hear you.'

It wasn't completely true: I could hardly hear anything. I had to raise my voice over Shona's anguish – as if yelling to Charlie in a hurricane.

'St Bartholomew's is closest. You need to take the Central

line two stops west. Two stops. To St Paul's, yeah? Then it's a short walk to Bart's. They'll sort you out there.'

Lowri said, 'Central line, two stops, St Paul's, St Bartholomew's.'

She said this firmly, and to herself, as a way of committing it to memory.

And I said, 'Thanks, man. Thanks a lot. Sorry about this. It was a pillar.'

I didn't admit that I'd marched her into it myself.

Charlie directed us down an escalator towards the Central line, and we found it without trouble, but there were two platforms to choose between. I checked the large map on the wall of the station, arranged vertically, showing all the various stops. I spotted St Paul's and pointed at it and motioned Lowri to hurry – *come on, a train's arriving* – as fusty air stirred around us, like the exhale of some giant prehistoric worm, and a headlight glinted out of the dark, followed by the crescendo-roar as the whole thing burst from the tunnel and shuddered to rest in front of us, the lament of its brakes momentarily blocking out Shona's screams.

The doors yawned wide and sucked us inside. I slumped into a seat and held Shona and rocked her and shushed her gently. Lowri came to stand over us, patting at Samuel – who had also begun mewling, frightened by the pain of his sister – and I assumed nobody would want to take the spot next to us, but a young woman with spiked green hair settled one seat over. She peered openly at Shona, whose cheek had swollen to twice its normal size. It looked like a spider bite inflamed with infection. Her wails now had form: 'My face, my face!'

'That looks bad,' the woman said.

'We're taking her to St Bartholomew's.'

I don't know why I said that, rather than 'the hospital'. It made it sound as if we were on a religious pilgrimage, taking our sick child to be healed. The woman made a sympathetic face and plugged in her headphones, cranking them, the screaming of raw punk rising like a chorus to Shona's pain.

As the train lurched into motion I continued to pat and soothe and rock her, without any real hope of calming her: it was an automatic gesture, something I had done on nights when she wanted Mom but Mom wasn't available. We stopped, the doors snapped open and shut, and as we started moving again I looked up at Lowri, her expression strained, and still tinged by suppressed accusation. I wanted to hold up my hands, admit to her and the whole carriage: it was my fault. I inflicted this hurt.

Then the tube was slowing again. The blurring outside the carriage wound down, bringing the world into focus, revealing a herd of people waiting to get on, and behind them the station sign: Mile End. I looked up to the tube map above the doors, mentally tracing the red Central line. Charlie had said two stops, which meant we should have been there.

I turned to the woman next to me to make sure.

'Does this train go to St Paul's station?'

She unplugged one earbud, shook her head. 'Other way.'

In my rush, somehow, I'd led us to the eastbound platform. I looked at Lowri, stricken, and stood up: passengers were shuffling on already, and of course staring at us: two sweaty parents, two screaming children, blood and tears and improvised bandages, all heading the wrong direction on the Central line. I emitted an urgent, frustrated sound and bulldozed through the mass of people crushing onto the tube, behaviour that might have provoked backlash in other circumstances.

I made it to the platform and stepped out just as the doors were closing, looked back to see Lowri gazing at me from the other side of the glass, both of us as mystified as animals in a menagerie. She shook her head, helpless, and I just shouted, 'I'll meet you at the hospital – call Bea!' before the train pulled away, taking my wife and son with it, and I was alone on some random platform with my wounded daughter.

I had been holding or carrying Shona for a quarter hour and my biceps had a constant muscle-burn. My skin prickled with heat and my shirt leeched to my back. I felt a steady, panicked pulse at the base of my neck. Shona's keening had shifted into a lower-pitched wailing. Mingling with it I heard music, so peaceful the contrast was dream-like: gentle drumming, and somebody singing about a knight in a book, and a worm on a hook. A song I knew, or should have known. I listened, dislocated. I found it hard to link up any kind of synaptic connection. Fortunately I didn't have to think hard, or in a complex way. I just had to get on a train going the other direction: to St Paul's, and St Bartholomew's.

The station had an overhead walkway, connecting the two opposing platforms. To go back, I had to get Shona up and over and down. I shifted her, holding her in a hug so that she could link her arms around my neck, and trudged up the steps to the walkway, haunted by the song, so faintly familiar but unfathomable. Something about all the things I'd done wrong.

As I descended the stairs on the other side I heard the

rumbling approach of a train, and attempted something I clearly shouldn't have, given that I was breathless and exhausted and moving on weak, gelatine legs and holding an injured child in my arms: I tried to hurry. I didn't run, exactly, but I quickened my steps and held Shona steady while I stomped and puffed downwards, as if working out on a StairMaster.

Only I couldn't see the stairs past Shona's head. On the second-to-last step I misjudged and my heel skidded off the lip and my leg shot out and I went down, unable to halt my momentum, toppling forward in a slow, absurdist manner, like a clown dying in pantomime, putting out an elbow to protect Shona, feeling the electric jolt in my funny-bone, the wrench in my shoulder, the jarring impact followed by stunned stillness.

I rested like that, half on my side, truly brought low, as the train wheezed to a stop and sucked open its doors and spat out passengers and swallowed up others. I didn't have it in me to stand, to get on, and as it pulled away I merely lay there clutching my daughter as if weathering a storm while people stepped over us, until somebody asked if we were OK.

Standing above us was a woman who had a long grey ponytail and a conga drum hanging from a strap around her neck: the busker who'd been playing.

'I'm going to St Bartholomew's,' I said, repeating my mantra.

'You've got to slow down,' the lady said.

She smelled of weed and was wearing a faded Isle of Wight Festival T-shirt and baggy cords. She had the same kind of confident serenity that I associated with Beatrice.

'Can you help me up?' I asked her.

She extended a hand, and I managed to haul myself upright without letting go of Shona, who was still sobbing, though no more so than before our tumble. I heard rattling and turned to look down the track: another train was arriving, only minutes after the first. It had been pointless to rush. As if to emphasize this, the woman nodded and resumed her song, the drumming languid and purposeful, and as we stepped on the train she hit the chorus line.

'Daddy,' Shona said, the word a whimper, 'Why is the bird on a wire?'

I told her I didn't know.

From there it was a long, morose tube ride back towards St Paul's. A teenager tapping away on his phone stood, offering us his seat without actually looking up from the game he was playing. I sank into the seat and Shona settled into a dull state of semi-shock on my chest and I continued

humming to her – carrying the lady's tune – as we swayed
back and forth to the rhythm of the tube, worming its way
beneath the city, winding and convulsing.

'It hurts,' Shona said, and whimpered.

I murmured commiserations, rested my chin on her
collarbone. I felt empty and resonant as the woman's drum,
which seemed to still pulse and echo in my skull. The
brooding resentment I'd carried – against Bea, for not being
able to visit us, and insisting we come to her; against Lowri,
for lagging behind, for not keeping up, for accepting our
parental fate – faded, replaced with impressions of my drive
down the motorway, my insistence we come in the first
place, my compulsion to prove something, to Bea, to Lowri,
to myself, to anybody, that we were succeeding as parents,
as people. My furious effort that had led my daughter into
a pillar, led me onto the wrong train, and nearly led to
another accident.

I kissed my daughter's head, stroked the soft swirl of hair
on the crown. 'Nearly there,' I murmured.

She didn't respond. I checked: her eyes were shut. She
could have been asleep, but she looked inert. I knew what
that meant. A concussion. She was unconscious. You had
to keep kids awake, alert, when they had a head injury.
Otherwise they could sink into a coma, as she clearly had.
I stood up, knocking my own head against the handrail on

the ceiling of the tube, and held her away from my body. 'Shona,' I said. 'Shona!'

Her face twisted up, and she grimaced at being disturbed. I'd never been so grateful to hear her cry.

By the time we reached St Paul's, she had sunk back into dozy somnolence, and I'd had about ten minutes' rest. My arms and legs were recharged. As we rolled up to the station I took a few steadying breaths, and stepped out onto the platform. I stood for a time taking stock, taking it slow. Signs further down the platform said *Way Out*, and other passengers gravitated towards them. I followed, one step at a time, hugging my daughter protectively, as if I'd rescued her from an earthquake or flood or burning building.

Together we rode up one escalator, and another. At the turnstiles I had to explain to the employee – a woman with wire-rimmed glasses whose nametag said 'Kerry' – that my wife had our tickets, but we'd been separated, and that I needed to get to St Bartholomew's.

Kerry had already clocked the blood, the wound, the trauma.

'Just so you know,' she said, 'they don't have A&E at St Bart's.'

'They better have something.'

She shrugged and gave me directions as complex as an algebra equation, which I nodded along to without really absorbing, needing to believe – with a kind of faith – that I would get us there and they would help us. When the directions finished I thanked her, as if I'd understood it all, and trudged up the stairs to the exit, and peered hopelessly down the street: a jumble of cars, pedestrians, construction cranes, concrete and glass – the usual city chaos – with me standing in the midst of it, looking for a sign, any kind of sign.

My phone started ringing. My brick of a phone that I had to keep in my jacket pocket, since it wouldn't fit in my jeans. I shifted my grip on Shona, trying to decide how to get at it, when I noticed a woman wearing a baby-carrier across the street, making a call.

Lowri.

I called her name, and again, until she caught sight of me. When the light changed she hurried across to join me; she had Samuel asleep on her chest. She'd arrived at the same time – maybe even on the same train – since she'd gotten off at the next station to double back.

'Can you find the hospital on your phone?' I asked.

'I already have: it's this way.'

'Let's take it slow.'

As we walked – both of us with a child on our chest – she leaned forward to get a look at Shona's face.

'How is she?' she asked.

'She stopped crying.'

'It's still bleeding.'

'That's why we're going to the hospital.'

St Bartholomew's was an impossibly old and imposing British building that looked like both monument and ruin. We had to pass through a two-storey gateway before approaching the hospital proper: brickwork and sandstone, arches and columns. The interior had been updated and modernized, but it retained the cold gravitas of a church or temple, as if we really had reached some site of pilgrimage. We huddled uncertainly in the main lobby, surrounded by patients, gurneys, staff in scrubs criss-crossing the space, until somebody – a young nurse with a surgical mask under his chin, like a frog's breathing sac – asked if we needed help.

We explained the situation, and though the hospital didn't have A&E it had a minor injuries unit. We made our way there, solemnly, through a labyrinth of corridors. We were assigned a number and collapsed into hard plastic chairs and waited amid other people with minor wounds, ailments, or injuries. Some were adults, but many were children: a girl with a dog bite; a boy whose finger had been crushed; a toddler who'd had a minor allergic reaction and looked all flushed and puffy. It made me feel strangely comforted, seeing those children and their parents. It wasn't only us. It was them, too. Or all of us, together.

Lowri was studying the wound critically.

'It's going to scar,' she said.

I'd only been thinking of the immediate hurt, and damage, and stitches. Not the long-term repercussions. Shona had such a delicate face. The thought of it being marked, forever, made something in me shrivel and wilt.

'I guess it will,' I admitted.

We sat in accusatory silence for another minute, until – finally – I told Lowri I was sorry, and she said, 'It wasn't your fault,' and I said that it was, that it usually was my fault.

'We don't need to stay in London,' I said. 'We don't have to see Bea.'

'I called her.'

'What did she say?'

'It was hard to hear. She was in one of her meetings.'

I sat back, gazing dismally at the doors. We hadn't seen Beatrice for a year and now likely wouldn't see her again for a few more. It shouldn't have mattered but it did: another misfortune to add to the day's calamity, and proof this whole endeavour I'd led us on had truly been a fool's errand. And even as I sat there, brooding about that, the doors to the waiting room opened and a tall woman in heels and a long jacket, with dark hair and dark sunglasses, strode in regally. I thought I was imagining her for a moment, and stood up.

'Beatrice!' Lowri called.

She had a shopping bag in each hand. She looked like a general striding into a field hospital, among the wounded: confident and commanding and ready to boost morale.

'What are you doing here?' I asked.

'Lowri called and told me what happened.' She removed her sunglasses and studied Shona critically. 'How is the little gremlin?'

Shona had woken up – either at me standing, or the sound of Bea's voice. She smiled sleepily. 'Auntie Bea,' she whispered, like an incantation.

'Come here.'

She dropped her bags and Shona slid willingly into her arms. 'Did you smash your face, little darling?' Bea said, in a Texan drawl. 'You must have been so brave.'

Shona admitted that she'd cried, but not too much. Bea sat and put her on her knee and produced an array of toys, which she had apparently picked up on the way or else had planned to give us at the museum. Some of the other kids wandered over, and Bea even had trinkets to hand out to them. It was like Santa Claus, or a saint, had descended on the ward.

'Don't you have meetings this afternoon?' I asked her.

'I cancelled them,' she said.

She teased and tickled Shona until she forgot about the hurt, and Bea cheered us up, too: she told us about her own childhood injury, how she had slipped in the bathroom and cracked her chin on the sink, splitting it to the jawbone. There'd been blood everywhere.

'Look,' she said, tilting her head up.

And she really did have a scar there – a thin white scar, curved like a crescent moon. She said she knew people now in LA who'd had such scars removed, but she never would. It gives a face character, she assured us, having a scar or two. We all need a few knocks, a few blemishes. It makes us tougher, and stronger.

'Isn't that right, darling?' she said to Shona. 'And you're a toughie, aren't you? A little super-girl. You're invincible.'

Shona jutted out her chin, solemn and determined, and so endearing that I had to look down, away – overcome – and I fumbled for my wife's hand and felt her squeeze my fingers in return, giving and forgiving, both of us able to believe, just for a moment, that it was true.

JUBILEE

Layla AlAmmar

June 2007

We never ride the train. Um Nadia says it's because it makes her sick, but she's lying when she says this. It's the crowds she can't deal with. The intimacy of strangers, of bodies pressing up against her or brushing past on their way to the exit or an empty seat. She doesn't like to be touched. Whenever we're in this city, with its lights and beings and things, she calls taxis to shuttle her from one place to another, even if they take longer or stink of fried food or charge an obscene amount for so short a journey.

I don't mind the crowds. I like the underground. It's an image of the world above, a microcosm that mimics what happens up there on those dense, pushy streets. The posh couple boarding at Notting Hill, with their jewels and brands and expensive smiles, making their way east or south. The men in suits with their important leather bags disembarking at Westminster. The boys who look like girls and girls who look like boys deboarding at Bethnal Green or Camden. The Bengalis heading east or the Africans crossing the river. The rich Arab tourists playing locals, as Dahlia and Nadia used to do, going from one shopping stop to another, leaving their mothers and aunties to taxi back and forth above them. It's all here, encapsulated in these metal tubes hurtling through space and time, day in and day out, forever.

There are only a handful of us here, spread out along the blue and white carriage for the sake of personal space. A beautiful young woman in business trousers and a cream blouse plays with her phone, a large diamond twinkling on her left hand. An olive-skinned man with a thick beard reads the newspaper, heavy black bag at his feet and low hat shading his eyes, the sort of man people might be concerned about were it not for the large wooden cross lying on his hairy chest. *I'm* the sort of man people might be concerned about were it not for my high-end clothes and clean face. There's a blond man with pale, almost white, eyebrows standing near the door, staring at it with a quiet intensity while the cellphone in his hand beeps out endless notifications. We sway here, in quiet communion, with the movement of the train.

I wonder where my girl is. Dahlia, with her sad eyes and mind that is still so very far away. She left the hotel early this morning, before her mother was awake. In a long sweater, despite the June heat, she grabbed her small shoulder bag, put on those massive sunglasses she never takes off and walked out of the suite. If Um Nadia is awake, she asks Dahlia unending questions about where she's going and who she's meeting. She cannot fathom someone wishing to just wander the city streets alone. She sees no value in it. Depending on her mood, she will cajole or guilt-trip our daughter into staying close, as though proximity to us is what guarantees her protection.

There are no guarantees in life. Certainly none of safety.

She gets it from me, her constant longing for solitude. I have always preferred my own company – in my garden at home, among the herbs and flowering shrubs and curious street cats, or in my study with Umm Kulthum on the stereo and maps spread open, circles on cities I plan on taking my family to next, or driving up and down the Gulf Road like those teenagers making eyes at each other at every stop light. Dahlia is like this, though now I wonder if it is a thing she inherited from me, like the curls in her hair or the point of her chin, or whether it is an acquired habit, born of what was done to her. If this tendency weren't so strong in me, would I have been more suspicious of it in her? Would it have compelled me to seek out a malign cause? Or would I have ignored it, accepting it as just another facet of her new personhood?

The train shudders to a stop and more people come on. It must be pouring outside because they are cursing the rain and the winds and the streets with their buses and cars crashing through puddles. Three young men get on, barely more than teenagers, and shake themselves like wet dogs, flinging huge droplets here and there and shoving at one another with cackles and filthy words. It's how my brothers and I were, a lifetime ago now, on our first trip to this city. There's a young family, a mother and father and two little boys. The children are in matching boots and raincoats and the woman with the diamond ring loves it, calling them over to sit by her and cooing over the outfits. The mother and father smile and look proud of these little lives they've created. She looks tired and uses her bony hands to crack her neck to the side, laughing when her husband shivers and winces in response. Another woman gets on, with a young girl dragging her feet and slumping into the seat at her side. The girl is all in black, with heavy black lines around her small eyes and blue dye streaking her hair and those heavy leather boots all the teenagers in this city wear, like they're always marching off to war.

This girl, twelve or thirteen, would she have caught his eye? She's a child, and a shiver crawls up my spine at the thoughts and images that crash, unbidden, into my mind. I am sick with it, or with the motion of the train, or with some combination of all that we have endured these past years.

Girls are terrifying creatures. Tiny, helpless beings that you carry around on your hip, who only want soft and pastel-coloured things, whose faces you have to wipe clean of their mother's make-up, and then suddenly, over a day and night it seems, they are something new. They become what you never expected them to be. Gone is the softness and the seeking of comfort from Mama's lap or Baba's shoulder. Instead, there is coldness and dark illustrations you can't begin to understand, and silence. So much silence and shoulder-shrugging and 'I'm fine'. What is a girl at twelve, at thirteen? She's like clay. She can be whatever you want, whatever she thinks she ought to be. The future is a prism, and she can throw herself into any light, any colour, any existence. There is no way to tell what the woman will be.

They say, when you are creating them, you are planting a seed, but the analogy ends there. There is the seed planted, but you have no idea what will grow – a flower, a tree, a cactus. There is no way to predict it. You can only wait and see.

Where is my girl? The minute they leave their mother, control becomes an illusion and their safety forever and always in question. Is she on the streets above me now, with the train rumbling, unfelt, beneath her feet? Are men leering at her, making obscene gestures and speaking terrible things? How often, and in how many ways, is she subject to the animalism of men? There is no way for me to shield her from everything – when I couldn't even shield her from *him* – no way to shove her back into her mother's womb, where she was, always, warm and safe.

The first time I rode the underground, back in the late Seventies or early Eighties, a man showed me his penis. That sounds like it was directed at me, which I don't think it was. It was more of a display for the whole train carriage. Two teenage girls sat across the aisle from the man and the large, semi-erect member rising from his gaping trousers. At first they were too preoccupied, giggling behind their palms, wrapped up in some saga from school. When they did see, they screamed with what sounded like two girlish squeals of delight – are these the things that confuse men who are monsters? The train stopped and the man ran off, and the girls chased after him, screaming, 'Get him! He's got his willy out!'

Did Dahlia ever consider being that brave? Did my girl ever, for one second, consider coming to me, telling me what he was doing to her? I cannot forgive her that silence. So many silences I brushed off – silences of moodiness, silences of a girl coming to terms with menstruation, silences of chemicals firing in a growing mind. But I cannot forgive the silence of hands wandering over her body, lips touching where they shouldn't have, attention from a man who should not have been giving it to her.

Dr Jamal told me when I, against Um Nadia's wishes, consulted a therapist about our daughter who never left the bed, who didn't eat, didn't speak, who would not look anyone in the eye, that I shouldn't blame her, that she felt guilt enough for what had happened to her. He said women were hard-wired to feel guilt, to take the blame for whatever misfortune befalls them. I said it was us men, with our failings and insecurities and inherent weakness, that caused them to feel that way. The doctor didn't agree, but neither did he argue. He said to let Dahlia go at her own pace and to hold my tongue around her.

I had nothing to say to her, least of all words of blame. She was a child. She *is* a child. It was him. It was all him. And it was me and her mother and the trust we so badly misplaced. The guilt is mine. The failure is mine, and it always will be.

I have no words of blame to direct at her, but deep down, in my heart, at times I can feel the emotion simmer and bubble.

I was full of rage then, when it happened. What father wouldn't have been? I thought I would kill him, my fury was so incandescent. It was a white-hot emotion, flaming behind my eyeballs. I felt lit up with it, zealous with it. I felt certain it would burn me up from the inside out, so that I would be left as nothing but a pile of useless ashes on the carpet.

It took months to douse the flames: months of Um Nadia and her pleas for silence to protect the family honour; months of watching Dahlia more closely than I've ever watched anything, on the lookout for pill-hoarding or sharp objects or anything else she might turn against herself; months of reading about that specific kind of trauma and how best to pull a loved one out of its grip. It took months, two years now, but still the embers are there in my belly. They refuse to die.

Perhaps they never will.

The train stops again, *KILBURN* passes before my eyes, and I try to place it on my mental map of the city, but I have ridden far beyond my normal neighbourhoods now, and I don't know it well enough. I try to gauge the area by the people who get on at this stop. It's not raining here, that much is obvious, as laughing twos and threes, dry and warm, board the car: two Asians, young, maybe Dahlia's age, with hat brims low over their eyes and patches on their shirts; a white man with fire engine hair moving his head in time with the beat coming out of his headphones, a tinny annoyance that scratches at my mind; an old couple, dry and wrinkled, he patient with hands clasped behind his back while she shuffles along to an empty seat. How can these trains run like this all day and night, carting all these lives around? Trains bursting with all manner of beings, so many people, all with stories, horrors, troubles and joys. All these people brimming with love, with hate, with fear and anxiety, how can the trains carry them all? The woman with her twinkling diamond ring disembarked at some point that I didn't notice, but the man with the white eyebrows remains at the door, glancing down at his phone and clenching his fist every so often in a tense motion.

When the girls were younger, I used to tell them there was a world parallel to our own, one inhabited by *jinn*, strange beings that were just like us but made of fire. Their world perfectly overlapped ours in every way: they had buildings and towers and bridges; they had families and friends and lovers; they were doctors and bankers and politicians and believers and infidels. Just like us, like how the underground mirrors the world above it. And that some places, like this city perhaps, were so full of beings, so full of all the world had ever and would ever contain, that it tore a piece of fabric in space and the *jinn* would come here to play.

Nadia would just laugh it off, but Dahlia's black eyes would grow huge and round in her little face and she would squeak out a 'Really?' or 'Swear, Baba!' And then, I would laugh and lift her into a hug. When she was older, she challenged me, saying that if what I said were true, we'd be able to play in the world of the *jinn* as well, and I'd wiggle my eyebrows and say, 'How do you know we don't?' and she would go very quiet and return to her ever more monstrous drawings.

At the time, I had thought it was these things, imaginary things, that scared her.

These days, Um Nadia, at night, when we are in bed and quiet, will try to talk to me about Dahlia marrying, as though this is something our daughter would ever now consider. I tell her it's impossible, that she is foolish and stupid for thinking of such a thing at this time, barely two years now since it happened. She disagrees, *'The best way for her to forget is to be married to a man who is good to her.'* As if finding such a man is as easy as going to the market for rice. I have no patience for these in-the-dark mumblings of hers. I turn away and pretend to sleep, barking at her when she talks about trips to Beirut or Cairo where a doctor can stitch our girl back to innocence. She cannot conceive of our daughter remaining innocent despite what was done to her. She thinks such a thing could stitch up the past or sew over what happened. Can this doctor stitch up our minds as well? Can he shut away the images and the dead look in her eyes and the memories that I sift through searching for some sign I'd missed?

She used to ask me if I regretted not having boys, if I was displeased with her for giving me two girls instead, as if it were in any way within her control. It took years for us to have any children at all, I didn't care what we ended up with. It took so long that I wondered whether it was right that we should have them, that perhaps God was sending us a sign that we were unfit for it. Um Nadia was hysterical, always talking this nonsense of my taking a second wife to supply me with children because 'What else is the point of marriage?'

I sometimes wonder if any of this is God's will, or if we forced the issue with children and are now being punished for it.

Nadia was perfection. Nadia was easy. She wanted pink and dolls and her mother's lap until she was fourteen or fifteen. There was no moodiness, no sullen mouths and hard eyes and silent shrugging of shoulders. She wanted a big wedding and a prince and babies to dress and cuddle and burp on her shoulder. She said yes to the first man Um Nadia presented her with, and in no time was eager to start pushing out babies of her own. Nadia lulled us into a false sense of security. Stupidly, we thought that since they were raised in the same house, by the same parents, in the same surroundings, Dahlia would be just as easy.

It tortures me, this not knowing how much of it was her and how much was what he was doing to her.

She thinks of it too. She said it once when she thought I wasn't listening, when she had her sketchbook open in her lap and she was drawing something so dark I asked her to put it away before her mother returned. She was pressing harder and harder into the lines, shading and darkening her ghouls and shadows, and I heard her mumble, *'There's a world somewhere where this didn't happen.'* It torments me all the more, that she is so aware of how utterly and completely her life has and will always be impacted by this.

He took more than her body, that monster. He took more than her body or her innocence or her trust. He took who she might have been.

The train stops at a station I recognize, but the majority of passengers are uninterested in it. I almost miss it, the doors are almost closing, but I lunge for the gap and keep them open with an arm and squeeze my way out. The man with the white eyebrows calls me a 'wanker' for holding up the train as the doors bounce back open and the conductor comes on to tell people not to block the exits. There's hardly anyone in the halls as I make my way through the station, but throngs of them are clogging up the lane heading for the eastbound platform. I don't know what time of day it is, or what the conditions are outside, and when I get to the main atrium, when I'm staring at those boards showing the tangled web of lines that will take you anywhere, I can't help but focus on the pink and yellow and purple ones heading for King's Cross. King's Cross and its trains that could take me anywhere – to the north, south, up and east. Or get back on the train I just scrambled off and go down to Waterloo to catch a train to Paris or Brussels. Take a train to anywhere, to nowhere. Escape this. All these lives I don't know what to do with any more.

It isn't raining any more, but the residue is there. Puddles in the street, drops of water shaking loose from the trees and sliding off awnings, wet pedestrians and cars beaded with water. People have umbrellas tucked into armpits and hoodies still up over their heads. The sun is shining, but cafés and restaurants are mistrustful and haven't brought their tables and chairs outside yet.

Just because the thing is done doesn't mean it's over.

How many worlds are there, out there, spinning? Worlds where someone wasn't hurt, where someone noticed something they should have seen and handled it, where lives weren't shattered and bodies weren't ripped apart. Worlds of *jinn*, worlds like the underground, overlapping and brushing up against each other, worlds just like ours but with the smallest of differences. A *jinn*-Dahlia who didn't stay silent and her *jinn*-father who did something about it. Do these worlds exist? Are there places, bursting-with-beings places, where the fabric tears and we can play there?

I turn the corner and see the back of the hotel. I don't know this city at all, or perhaps I know it too well. On a bench in the little park across the way sits my girl in her too-heavy sweater with the sleeves pushed down to cover the scars on her pale arms. Under her fingernails, there will be candlewax. Under her eyes, there will be dark circles. There will be no expression on her face, and her mind will be very far away.

Does she not wander these streets, as I thought she did? Does she leave the hotel every morning just to sit in this park at its back? Does she do it out of fear, because she knows we're nearby should she need us?

What use is there for fear now, when the worst has already happened?

VICTORIA

Green Park

Janice Pariat

Every weekday, Elsa travelled north up the Victoria line. At nine, she'd leave the house she shared with three flatmates on Ferndale Road and walk out in a woolly coat regardless of the time of year. It was always cold on this island. She'd walk to Brixton tube station, which she thought looked like an entrance to a nightclub, and make her way to the platform. Across from her, every so often, a new advert loomed large. The latest, slimmest smart phone, short courses at the London College of Fashion, three-night holidays from £539, and today, a woman in a shimmery pink dress, bent over, smiling at her from between impossibly long, bare legs. 'Wax on wax off,' the poster declared. 'Your favourite salons at your fingertips!' Her fingertips, thought Elsa, mostly sported bitten-through nails, but she'd kicked that terrible habit. Well, almost.

She stopped, or changed trains, along the Victoria line depending on where her temp agency was sending her for the day, the week, the month. Even with her Literature degree, earned in Warwick, it had been difficult to find something permanent. It was difficult for mostly everyone these days. She interned at a few publishing houses, hoping they'd love her and keep her, wading through the *Annotated Elizabeth Gaskell* and books on gardening, but her time with them ended quietly and without ceremony. It also made her no money.

So now she did anything. A fortnight making phone calls to patients from an NHS No Smoking Service clinic. A few weeks at Oxford Circus sorting files for a man who transported art around the world. A month at Brixton Blockbuster, where she stacked VHS tapes and DVDs and tried not to silently judge people for the movies they were renting. (The one perk, though, was the free DVDs; she'd watch them in her room or occasionally with her flatmates – Alice, the girl from Italy, Ulla from Finland, or Eirik from Norway.) Then there was the data-entry job at an office in Pimlico run by three French people – two men and a woman, all tall and well dressed and soft spoken. She couldn't figure out why but she'd never felt more aware of her height (short) and her clothes (inexpensive). Worse, they spoke little English, so Elsa spent a week feeling that every time they conversed they were talking about her. Most recently, she'd spent three weeks at a university alumni office in Pentonville, making a million photocopies, and pasting stamps on envelopes carrying letters urging donations. It had been mercilessly dull.

Today, she was on her way to Highbury, to an artist's studio.

The day before, at the agency, she'd been apprised of her duties by Katie, the plump, petite girl at the recruitment desk.

'She wants me to do what?'

'Water her plants.'

They looked at each other in silence.

'For a month,' Katie added helpfully.

A while ago, at this, a sudden rage would've flared inside Elsa. She hadn't spent months, no, years, studying for *this*. Burdening herself with a student loan. Acquiescing to her parents' offerings of money to help with the rent so that she could stay here in London.

Now, Elsa asked briskly, 'How much?'

'Fifteen an hour.'

With that Elsa nodded and pocketed the spare key.

And so here she was, bag, lunch sandwich and book in hand, on her way to Highbury. She was glad it would take almost half an hour to get there. Given she found a seat, she liked tube journeys. Not too much of the city felt like it belonged to her, but in that carriage, in that pocket of time, somehow everything became hers. Her phone lost signal, her head quietened, and all the world narrowed to the rocking of the train, to the music on her headphones, or the book she was reading. At the moment, Mitchell's *Cloud Atlas*. Her mother had pressed it into her hands the last time she was home. And while she wasn't sure she was enjoying it when she started – so slow, she thought, and confusing – she was beginning to lose herself in it now. The stations flashed and rumbled past – Vauxhall, Pimlico, Green Park, Oxford Circus – and she barely noticed where she was until King's Cross. She got off at the stop after, striding out, crossing the road to Highbury Fields. It was October, already cold and blustery. Today wasn't the sunniest, but still the trees shimmered with a low, clear light. The studio stood atop one of the houses on the Crescent. She found it easily enough and let herself in. The place was immaculately white, with tall windows shaded by Venetian blinds, and bare hardwood flooring. Everywhere hung the smell of stone dust. Katie had mentioned Maria was a sculptor. What Elsa supposed was the living room was taken up by Maria's work and materials, tools scattered across long tables and smaller rotating stands. She gaped at the sculptures – gigantic headless figures with wings.

The plants were everywhere.

Large tropical ferns, boxes of herbs, smaller indoor leafy

pots Elsa was certain her mother could name but she couldn't. On the window sills, rows of turgid succulents. In the corner, on a circular table, a cluster of shiny terrariums. This would take her a while. As instructed, she looked for the watering can in the kitchen, and filled it carefully. She'd also been told she was welcome to make herself some tea, so when she finished, she did. She put the kettle on in the kitchenette, and eventually settled, with a cup and sandwich, in the only armchair in the room.

It was nice here, she had to admit. Definitely different from the cramped quarters she shared, where people constantly fell over each other in the kitchen, the hall, the bathrooms. Where someone always left dirty dishes in the sink, and stole her cheese or a tablespoon or two of Nutella. She was fond of her flatmates, she supposed, but in the time she'd been there, they had tended to come and go at an alarming rate. It was easier to be polite, mildly friendly, and not be too surprised if they packed up and left without saying goodbye.

It might have been the warmth inside, the comfortable armchair, but when she tried reading she found the book was making her sleepy. So, she put it away, and walked around inspecting Maria's work. The finished pieces stood to one side against the wall. An army of tall, dark angels.

Just then her phone rang, startling her. It would probably be her mum. Or one of her friends from university. But it wasn't. The number on her screen was unknown.

'Hello?'

On the other end, a terribly garbled voice. She moved to the window.

'Hello?'

Someone, a man, asking if she was Philip.

'Um . . . no.'

He asked for Philip again.

'Sorry,' she said, 'wrong number.'

Later, on her way back to the station, Elsa was beset with a strange restlessness. It was dark already. The evenings now falling faster. She thought a walk might do her some good but she didn't know the area well. Something disquieted her. She wasn't sure what or why.

Wasn't she . . . doing well?

They came back to her, the words of a therapist she'd once seen for a few sessions. 'When were you last happy?' Many times, she thought. An impulsive trip with friends to Mexico. In an old boyfriend's bed, waking up next to him in the morning. Watching The Black Crowes perform on stage. A university trip to Scotland a few summers ago.

No, she could hear Doctor Moresi say, think of a time when you were happy by yourself.

This was a struggle. Christmas with her family, perhaps. A trip to Greece with her mum. But entirely on her own?

Then it would have to be India.

On her solo six-month stay at a rural school in Tamil Nadu, teaching children art. It sounded like such a cliché that she almost laughed aloud. Then her few days in Delhi, in the winter, when the ruins of the city lay before her bathed in gold.

Good, this is good, Doctor Moresi encouraged, in her head.

She hadn't known anyone in Delhi, and everyone back home was petrified about her – 'so unsafe' – but she managed to navigate the city on her own. It was one of the few times Elsa had felt proud of herself.

The station was busier now, but she managed to find a seat, between a man in a grey suit and uncomfortable-looking pointy shoes and a woman in a tiger-print faux fur coat. They were both staring into their phones.

She'd used the Metro in Delhi too. Newly opened, spiffily clean and air conditioned, miles better than the London Underground, she'd told her family, laughing, over the phone. 'But it's over a hundred years old,' her father had protested. She couldn't recall the names of any of the stations, but she'd liked it, sitting in the women-only compartment. There was less staring there, she'd imagined, though more than a few curious glances were cast at her obvious unbelonging. It was sad that a city needed segregated carriages, she thought, but she liked to imagine it as an island, floating, Sappho on Lesbos. She told herself to stop being fanciful.

Back to Mitchell, to London, to the rhythmic rocking of the train, to seats that smelled of damp and dust.

The next time she was on her way to Highbury, it happened.

That thing at the station.

At only one station.

Elsa glanced up from her book. They'd stopped, and were about to pull away, the doors having shut noisily like sluice gates, and something outside, on the platform, caught her eye. But then they were gone, hurtling through the darkness, swaying. Was that Green Park? Or Pimlico? She wasn't sure. Maybe she'd imagined it. Besides, it was more a flash of something. Like a scene spliced into a film from another movie. On the way back, she was crushed in the centre, dangling by the handrail, and couldn't see beyond the crowd pressing into her.

A few days later, Elsa was on the tube again.

She looked up when they stopped at Vauxhall, because the doors closed and then opened again to allow someone in. Everyone sat silently impatient. The same happened at Green Park. But it was empty there. At least on the stretch she could see. No one standing on the open platform.

The open platform.

That was it. There were no open platforms here, certainly not at any stations along this stretch of the Victoria line. There were walls, mostly tiled in white, the red-circled sign, and backlit rectangles of advertising. They were at Warren Street by now, so Elsa couldn't check, but she was certain, like the last time, that she hadn't glimpsed solid wall and benches. Maybe there had been some recent renovations, she told herself. Drastic expansions. No, that seemed highly improbable.

Later that evening, when she was done at the studio, Elsa met a university acquaintance at a nearby pub. A couple of pints turned to many. She left feeling a little giddy, flushed to her cheeks. It was late, and a light drizzle was falling. People rushed past her, hands deep in their pockets, sunk into their coats against the cold. By now, at this hour, in this weather, the trains were running almost empty. She swayed along, the few people in her carriage stepping out at King's Cross. A teenage couple sat in the corner, kissing.

How was she so alone?

She tried recalling Doctor Moresi's instructions. 'When were you last happy?' No, when were you happy by yourself? Oh fuck it.

She leaned back, resting her head against the seat; it made her slightly nauseous, but she was tired, so tired, the weariness of the past few months swooping over her all at once like a flock of birds.

When she awoke, the carriage was in darkness. The train unmoving between stations. She sat up, her head woozy. And then the lights flickered back on. The couple in the corner were gone. A woman on her phone sat a few seats down across from her. How strange to be here, in an airlock, a capsule stuck in space. Cut off from the world. Then the train shuddered, and started.

They came back to her now. Her memories of India. How she wanted to return to the school where she'd volunteered, determined not to be one of thousands who assuaged their guilt for a few months on their gap year, promised the kids they'd come back, and then didn't. Next time, she'd visit a fort, any fort, and ride a camel. Which would mean Rajasthan, she'd thought happily. Of course, Tamil Nadu was way south . . . which meant she'd have to take a flight to Delhi . . . where she could stay a few days, and wander. The Red Fort and Humayun's Tomb. The Qutub Minar and the Lotus Temple. She saw herself walk the streets of the old city again. *I can't believe I did it all on my own.* She'd fancied herself a brave explorer.

The next week, on her way up to Highbury, Elsa decided she would look out at every stop. She hadn't slept well the night before, and would've liked to catch a nap, but she was determined. She was also certain nothing would be amiss. That every station would be as it always was. Honestly, she thought, she needed to get her eyes checked. Or her head. But she couldn't bear going back to see Doctor Moresi, that stuffy little office with the plastic flowers at the window, the tiny desk, the wooden chair.

Then at one station, everything was different. Again.

This time she saw it. Clear as day, except there was no sunlight down here, underground. Gone were the white-tiled walls, the benches, the advertisements, the large map of the London Underground. In their place, a wide-open platform, with angular pillars, and potted plants. Just before the train moved on, she glanced at the sign. It read 'Green Park'. And the next one they stopped at was Oxford Circus as usual. Elsa wanted to say something, to someone, anyone, but felt she'd lost her voice. Although it wasn't something she could enquire of people – 'Excuse me, did you see how that station didn't look anything like it's supposed to?' Batty, as her grandmother would say, pure batty.

She hurried through her chores at the studio, not pausing for her usual cup of tea. On the train, she sat and held *Cloud Atlas* open in her hands, but the pages remained unturned. Around her, to her side and across, rows of faces bent over phones and books and newspapers. A child at the far end was wailing; the mother looked young and stressed and embarrassed. At King's Cross, a sea of people in, a sea of people out, in waves. They travelled through the heart of the city, down south, towards the river, and under it. It startled her, the thought. How did one dig under a river? Just as one digs under the sea? What if somewhere along the line there were fissures? Soon, they came to Green Park. The train stopped, the doors wheezed open, and she was the only one who stepped out.

It was very quiet. And empty.

And apart from the name of the station, everything else was changed. It smelled different. Warmer, somehow. And the air seemed strangely hazy. To her left, the platform continued for a bit and then ended with a sign beyond which only 'Authorized Personnel' were permitted.

To her right, the platform travelled much further away to a staircase and escalators. The floor was a cool, gleaming grey, reflecting the lights that shone from a high vaulted ceiling. A yellow line, that people weren't meant to cross, ran along the edge of the platform. She glanced at the digital signboards above, but they stayed blank. Up ahead, she could see a white-faced clock, with the hands resting at half-past twelve. Had it stopped? When she'd stepped into the train at Highbury, it was about seven in the evening. But this . . . this seemed so unlike London. It felt impossibly like another city. She looked around for some sort of indication. The exit signs listed unfamiliar names. She was definitely elsewhere. But this was silly. She should just head outside and check. She walked the length of the platform to the stairs, but drawn across the top was a grille gate, locked.

She turned back, now beginning to wonder how she would make it out of here, or rather back on a train to Brixton. For a while she stood behind the yellow line and waited. Nothing swept past her. A slow panic crept across her chest. Was this an abandoned train station? She'd read about those. How they were closed from disuse, or a change in plan and layout. But this didn't look old, or dilapidated. In fact, it was shiny new, and somehow familiar. As though she'd been here before.

But for now, she needed to find a way out. Who knew if this station would ever open? It wasn't the pleasantest of plans but there seemed to be little else for her to do but hop off the platform, pick a direction, and walk along the tracks. Hopefully she'd come to a station that was open, or meet someone there who could help. She began stepping down, but instead of lowering, her foot touched floor.

Shaky, swaying, moving floor, flanked by seats, with a press of people sitting, standing around her. White people, and brown, commuter faces she'd never seen before but knew all too well. Only on the London Underground, she thought, could someone materialize out of nowhere in a carriage and have no one notice.

'Where's this train headed?' she asked her closest co-passenger, a tall man in a heavy grey coat.

'Brixton,' he muttered.

Well, she thought, that hadn't been too difficult.

She found a seat and, automatically, reached for her book, but it wasn't there. She'd left it behind.

Elsa went back for it the next day.

At about eleven in the morning, after rush hour. The train seemed slower, crawling from one station to the next. Every delay momentous. By Victoria she was waiting impatiently by the door. One stop later, she stepped out. This time into a swell of people on the platform, rushing out or standing, waiting for their train. Like last night, the air hung hazy. The lights gleamed white and bright. She glanced at the clock; it was almost four.

For a moment she stood amidst the bustle, unsure what she should do. What if she spoke to someone? Was all this real?

She walked up to a woman wearing a long red skirt, tapping into her phone.

'Excuse me . . . where am I?'

The woman looked up, unfazed – 'Yellow line' – and resumed messaging.

If nothing else, at least Elsa was certain it wasn't the Victoria blue.

Every now and then a beep and an announcement over the loudspeakers. A train arriving at platform one. Another departing from platform two. The destination boards held unfamiliar names, most of which she couldn't pronounce, until one flashed 'Kashmere Gate'. *That* she knew. She'd once got off there to visit the Red Fort, in the north of Delhi. In her heart stirred a small panic, a small happiness. Perhaps she could make her way there again. Walk along its ramparts, sit by its fountains, wander the hundred-pillared hall. But first, she thought, she should look for her book. She traced her way back, jostled by the crowd, hoping it would still be on the bench. It was, but it had been picked up by someone with cropped hair, wearing dangly earrings, and an outsized T-shirt.

She was sitting cross-legged on the bench.

'Hi . . .' said Elsa, 'I think that's mine . . .'

The girl glanced up. 'You think or are you sure?'

She was sure. But didn't wish to seem presumptuous. 'My name's on the first page . . .'

'I believe you. Here . . .'

The book was safely back in Elsa's hands.

'Fifty pages in and not a single spaceship.'

'Sorry?'

'Those are the only kind of books I read.'

'He's not that kind of sci-fi writer . . .'

'I figured.' The girl was smiling. 'Are you always this serious?'

'No,' said Elsa defiantly.

'Good . . . OK, here's my train . . .' And with a wave, she was gone.

Elsa began stopping regularly at Green Park station on her way back from the studio in the evening. When it was quiet on the Yellow line and she felt as though the whole world could be kept at bay. She couldn't do much; she read and sometimes lay on one of the benches staring at the ceiling. She should bring out her old pair of roller blades, she thought, and then laughed out loud at the ridiculousness of it all. She started coming on other days too, when she wasn't required at Islington or elsewhere. On some days, she timed it to catch the mad bustle of the evening rush. She'd sit almost unnoticed. Apart from a few young men who'd cast a quick interested glance in her direction. Before her, and behind, trains came and went, spilling their insides and being refilled again. It was comforting, the steady rumble and squeak of brakes, the whooshing of doors, the clatter of footsteps.

She wondered if she'd see the girl again.

She wished to, even if she couldn't quite explain why. She liked her. The way she seemed to be at ease and . . . autonomous. Maybe one day she would cut her hair that short. And dye it black. And wear large T-shirts and spangled earrings. And be an entirely different person. Once, she thought she saw the girl hopping into a carriage, but she was probably mistaken. What were the chances of crossing paths again in a place such as this?

Then one evening, the girl *was* there, cross-legged on the bench. They smiled at each other, Elsa shyly, in happy recognition.

'Where are you going?' the girl asked.

'Nowhere.' Elsa liked that she didn't seem to think this a strange answer. 'And you?'

'Where I always go.' She said she took the train at this

time almost every evening. 'But I like sitting here until the crowds lessen.'

'Yes . . . me too . . .'

'There's something about waiting in places which you're meant to leave.'

Elsa nodded, and added, 'Temporary places for temporary people.'

'Yes,' said the girl, 'that's exactly it.'

The next evening, the girl was carrying a small leaf-plate of snacks.

'Here.' She shoved it into Elsa's hands.

'What's this?'

'Ram ladoos.'

'What?'

'Pakodas . . . oh, I don't know . . . deep-fried lentil balls.' With grated radish and mint. Delicious.

'What train do you usually catch?'

'Whichever one happens to be passing by,' answered Elsa truthfully. She decided to try to tell the girl. 'I'm not from here, you know.'

'Yes, I can see that.'

'No . . . I mean . . .'

'What?' She was looking at Elsa with kindness.

Even in her head, though, it sounded too mad. 'Nothing, really . . .'

The girl hopped off the bench. 'You know, it doesn't matter . . .'

Elsa said she hoped so.

In return, one evening she brought some roasted chestnuts from a farmer's market she crossed on her way to the tube station. They sat round and barely warm in the paper bag.

'What are these?' the girl asked.

'Eat them quickly . . . before they get cold.'

For a while they sat in silence, cracking the shells, slipping the chestnuts into their mouths.

'You really aren't from here, are you?'

Elsa shook her head. 'But I've been here before . . . seems a lifetime ago.'

'And you keep coming back?'

'Now, yes.'

'Why?'

'Because it's easier . . . than being anywhere else.'

'What was it that Mitchell says . . .?'

Elsa looked at the girl in some surprise.

'There's a line in your book . . . every nowhere is some-where.'

'I like him.'

The girl agreed. 'He's a hopeful chap.'

A particularly packed train stopped before them. Barely anyone got out; in the carriage, through the glass, a close press of heads and bodies.

'I don't feel like leaving yet.'

Elsa said neither did she.

'It's a nice evening . . . shall we step out?'

All this while Elsa hadn't because she was afraid that while she was gone, something might happen which would make it impossible for her to return. She'd been tempted, of course, but hadn't yet gathered the courage. The girl was standing, waiting.

'What happened?' she asked.

'Nothing.' Elsa smiled. 'Would an Oyster card work here?'

'Let's find out.'

They walked along the platform, to the stairs. The gate at the top was drawn back, open. Over the loudspeaker, an announcement. Somewhere, the clank of traffic. Around them the sound of lives, moving.

METROPOLITAN

My Beautiful Millennial

Tamsin Grey

1.

It's a Friday halfway through December, my day off from my shit job. I've got a cold, and would have languished in my lumpy, scratchy bed, but Paul Fildes has summoned me to Amersham. He wants to have a discussion about Christmas, but not over the phone, because he finds our phone calls impossible. When I fall silent, it's like I'm howling in pain, and he can't reach me.

I take ages getting dressed, i.e. even longer than usual. I have finally gone for my black velvet dress with the flouncy skirt, bottle-green tights and my lace-up boots. Amethyst lipstick. My strange curly hair in spikes. My Napoleon coat, black beret, black leather gloves. My green carpet bag, yes, the same green as my tights. Paul Fildes says I wear 'dressing-up' clothes, that it's a sign of my arrested development. He has offered to take me shopping, for a suit, blouses, interview clothes. It would be fun to try things on in classy boutiques instead of charity shops, but I'm trying to disentangle myself from Paul Fildes.

Leaving my room in disarray, I creep out of the house that I share with around five other humans. (As they're mainly invisible, I can't be more precise.) It's biting cold, with a rose-gold sun throwing long black shadows. I pick up my wages from Mingles, and head for Aldgate. Outside the station a man in a gold paper crown is holding out a white paper cup. He has decorated his dog with tinsel, and the dog is all agitated, shaking and pawing himself, trying to get the stuff off. I drop a twenty-pence piece into the man's paper cup. He frowns.

'Is that all you can afford, love?'

Totally thrown, I dig in my bag for the brown envelope I've just been given, which I know contains ten twenty-pound notes, which I'm planning to hand over to Paul Fildes, and two tenners, which need to last me a whole week.

'Joking!' He's laughing, putting his hand over mine, to stop me opening the envelope. I flee into the station.

The Metropolitan line is a maroon colour, and Paul Fildes and I are marooned on either end of it. The train is waiting, silent and stately. I'm the first one on, and it feels like I'm spying on a secret world. Each way, the walk-through carriages, on and on, repeating themselves, the yellow poles, the yellow nooses, and the black strips saying *AMERSHAM, AMERSHAM, AMERSHAM*. Amersham is the resting place of Ruth Ellis, the last woman in Britain to be hanged. I know this because the last time I went to Amersham, Paul Fildes took me to see Ruth's grave.

I cringe, and sit down, putting my bag on the seat next to me, and as I pull off my hat and gloves I remember the cup man's raw, chapped fingers, and cringe again. I kind of hate him, and hate myself for hating someone who's slipped through the cracks and hung onto his sense of humour. The train starts moving, and I gaze up at the yellow nooses, rehearsing my speech to Paul Fildes.

'*You have been so kind . . .*'

'*You are a wonderful, generous person, and I know that . . .*'

'*Paul, I need to be straight with you . . .*'

Paul Fildes is the only person I've got to know since I moved to London, which was in the spring, after I got the all-clear, and my hair more or less covered my head. I could have gone back to uni, but all my friends had already left, and it would have been too weird, starting all over again. I met him on a personal development weekend, which my mum paid for as my twenty-first birthday present. She left her job to look after me, and has hardly any money herself, so it was generous of her, but I *so* would have preferred the cash. There were about twenty people on the course. Paul

Fildes stood out, being very tall and wide, with a great moon of a face, adorned with a bushy moustache. At the end, when everyone else was hugging and kissing, and I was standing there wondering if I was allowed to go home, Paul Fildes took me to one side and told me, very fervently, that he had a wealth of experience, and valuable contacts, and would like to support me to achieve my full potential.

'It's not that I don't like *you* . . .'

Do I like him? I think of his eyes, violet-coloured and thickly lashed, startling out of that great jowly face. On the personal development weekend he told everyone that his mother used to call him her 'little monster'. He also said that he was walking wounded from a relationship with a clinically depressed woman called Joy. He'd been a City boy, but had given that up because she needed twenty-four-hour attention. He'd supported her financially, through day trading, had carried her through five long years. He had got nothing back. It would be a long time before he was ready to risk intimacy again.

He wasn't anything like my idea of a City boy. But what did *I* know? On our first date – which I didn't realize was a date – he took me to the Dutch Pancake House in Holborn, and for a split second I was disappointed, but then decided it was an *ironic* place to have lunch. I hadn't drunk for a long while, so the house red went straight to my head. I didn't tell him about being ill, but I told him all my other secrets, including that I hated my mum's new boyfriend, that I was thinking of joining an escort agency, oh, and that I had voted Leave in the EU referendum.

He wasn't interested in my Brexit vote, said he hadn't bothered himself, as it wouldn't make any difference to people like him. I babbled on, telling him how I'd thought of leaving the EU as taking the road less travelled: as an adventure, a mystery, something wild and free. And then I'd realized that it was the opposite: that we were walling ourselves up, shutting things out; burying ourselves alive. I got carried away, half-knowing I was talking crap, and using my hands too much, until I knocked over my glass, and some wine dripped onto Paul Fildes's pale cavalry twill trousers. He tutted, and dabbed with his serviette, and said not to worry, these things happen. I passed him the water jug, and told him how nervous I was of people finding out, and thinking I must be a rustic racist.

'You live in fear of the vicious judgement of others.' He poured a drop of water onto the stain, shaking his head. 'Poor Dido.'

I laughed, feeling confused, and then asked why Brexit wouldn't affect people like him, and he put the jug down and said that he didn't want to talk about politics, he wanted to talk about *us*. And reached for my hand.

I snatched mine away. I was taken aback, because of what he'd said about needing to recover from Joy, and also because he is a *lot* older than me. But in a drunken muddle I wondered if I'd misread him, whether he was just being, I don't know, avuncular. Worried I'd been rude, I quickly passed him another serviette, trying to make it look as if that was why I'd moved my hand.

He said that he didn't think I should go into escorting. From what he understood of that industry, it wasn't just about going out to dinner. He looked hard at me to see if I'd got what he was driving at. I said that I wasn't under any illusions. He nodded, full of unspeakable emotion. To change the subject I asked him about day trading, and he groaned under his breath, and then asked for the bill. I asked what was wrong, and he suddenly exploded. 'Dido, you tell me you are going to prostitute yourself. And then you ask me about day trading. What am I meant to *make* of you?'

I felt too upset to answer. Like I'd blown it, that he wouldn't want to have anything more to do with me. But once he'd paid, he seemed to pull himself together. He looked at his watch, and then out of the window, and gazed at me thoughtfully for a while. Then he said he hoped very much I would let him lend me some cash. It would be his pleasure, and he would be in no hurry to be repaid. 'I'm practically a baby boomer, Dido,' he said. 'And you . . .'

He reached over and took my jaw in his giant fingertips. '. . . are my beautiful millennial.'

I borrowed £200, and saw him a lot over the summer. He took me to the British Museum to see the mummies, to a very *long* foreign film at the National Film Theatre, and for a disgusting breakfast in the Best Western Hotel. I sent a snap of him to my friend Chloe, with the title *SUGAR DADDY*, but it wasn't like that. We kissed hello and goodbye (on the lips, mine firmly closed, his slightly parted). He never tried to take my hand again, but we brushed against each other surprisingly often. He would quiz me on whether I'd started therapy, or seen a spiritual healer, or written an angry letter to my mother, but I'd always failed to follow up any of his recommendations. He told me I was 'obstinate', 'evasive', 'complex', 'damaged', and also 'bewitching'. I took to teasing him, to lighten the mood, and to begin with he was perplexed, but he gradually understood, and one day he threw back his head and chortled. It was kind of like when a baby first laughs, apart from not, because instead of joy and wonder it filled me with a deep foreboding. He started trying to tease me back, but the best he could manage was these awful, priggish put-downs which made my blood run cold.

I kept seeing him, but I longed for people my own age, people who could do real banter, who knew who Ed Sheeran was, and could discuss crisp flavours. In September, at his insistence, I trekked out to Amersham. His bungalow, on the edge of a cul-de-sac, smelt of socks, and the remains of a kebab strewn under his two giant day-trading screens. There was one picture, a photograph of a ballerina. 'My mother,' he said, and hesitated, but said no more and I didn't like to ask. We got the bus to Old Amersham, which was all cobbles and timber, but with a Costa, and a Tesco's, and a Joules. In the graveyard he showed me where Ruth Ellis is buried. It's just a grassy patch, with nothing marking it, and he told me how Ruth's son Andy destroyed the headstone with a hammer, just a few days before taking his own life. Andy had been ten when his mother was hanged, for shooting her racing driver lover dead outside the Magdala pub in Hampstead. As he told me about Andy, he reached for my hand again; and paralysed by the sadness, I let him hold it.

2.

The pigeon gets on at Baker Street. I'm thinking about Paul Fildes, rehearsing what to say to him, and I haven't been following the starts and stops and comings and goings. I am vaguely aware of the teenager sitting opposite – that he's black, that he's dressed in black, with white trainers, and white wires coming out of his ears. And also the white woman doing her make-up, the way she's spread her kit out on the seat next to her, her silver fur coat, and her fountain of cream soda hair. I've taken in these two, and the bright red scarf of a man sitting further along, and a sad-eyed woman with a suitcase and two listless small children. I don't register the pigeon until it's right by my feet, bobbing and bustling, and I scream, I can't help it, and clutch my knees into my chest. And then I feel like a total idiot.

The boy opposite looks at me, and then the pigeon, and then back at his phone. No one else takes any notice, out of indifference, or politeness, who knows. I put my feet back down firmly, asserting myself over the pigeon. It's a battered-looking thing, lopsided, with petrol-sheened feathers and mangled feet. It holds its space, examining me with first one tiny orange eye and then the other. Trying to ignore it, I blow my nose, and then fix on the cream soda woman's application of mascara. It's weird, people doing their make-up on the tube. Such an interesting thing to watch, and they're doing it right there, right in front of you, but you feel like you should pretend it's not happening. Aware of the pigeon, I look at the man in the red scarf, a white man, peaky-looking, and he's wrapped the scarf across his nose and mouth like he's worried about breathing in germs. He looks familiar, but I don't know why. The ends of the scarf are tucked into his camel overcoat, underneath which he's wearing jeans, and brown Chelsea boots. His legs are crossed, which is unusual, for a man on the tube, and very thin, too thin to be wearing skinny blue jeans. I look back up at his face, and it dawns on me that he's a famous actor. I can't remember his name, but he might have been Dr Who for a while. As I study him, his eyes suddenly slide to meet mine, hostile, and I quickly look away. The pigeon seems to have moved closer, and my muscles tense, and, completely by mistake, I look back at the actor, who notices, and I want to die. Everyone else is oblivious to him, even the listless children, because they are *real* Londoners, default setting '*Whatever*', not wide-eyed Brexit-voting bumpkins like me. Then I realize that some-one's talking, I can hear the sound of it but not the words, and I see that it's the man in the orange puffer jacket. Guantanamo Bay orange, is what comes to me. He's partially hidden by the silver fur shoulder of the cream soda woman, so I can see a portion of the jacket, and his face, which is olive-skinned, his moving lips and his black curly hair. I watch his lips, trying not to remember that muttering is one of the signs of a suicide bomber. If I was a Londoner I wouldn't be so jumpy, I wouldn't be so racist,

I wouldn't be such a total jerk. But he's staring at his lap, and a fixed stare is another sign. Does he have a rucksack? I lean to my left, away from the pigeon, pretend to be looking in my bag. He *doesn't* have a rucksack, and he *isn't* just muttering to himself, but reading aloud from a book. He darts me a look, *not* hostile, questioning, and I fumble in my bag, pretending I didn't actually look at him at all. And then, as I straighten, the pigeon rushes at me, headlong, and I scream again, and I flap my feet at it, to ward it off, but the toe of my boot makes contact, and, with a hoarse and terrible whistle, it rises a foot into the air, and then plummets back to the floor.

'Fuck's sake . . .' The teenager pulls the plugs from his ears and peers at the pigeon. I notice the children looking too, with slack, incurious faces. The actor is looking at his fingernails.

'I'm so sorry,' I say to the boy.

'Don't say sorry to *me*.' The boy is watching the pigeon, who is back on its feet, but distinctly unsteady.

'I didn't – do you think it's OK?'

The boy shrugs. Everyone gazes after the pigeon, who is pluckily hobbling up the aisle. Then the boy puts his earplugs back in, and the reading man goes back to his book, and the celebrity sinks further into his scarf. It's only me watching the pigeon hobble along the train. I wonder if I should go after it, gather it up, pop it in my bag and take it to the nearest vet. How much would it cost, to mend a pigeon? Would the money in my bag be enough? The pigeon has turned round, is coming back, is picking up speed. I try to stay calm, to be in the moment; I close my eyes and listen to the reading man's lovely voice. But I know the pigeon is coming back to take revenge, and when I take a peek it's right there, in front of me, its orange eyes blazing. And then, in a flurry of feathers it takes off, its beak aimed right at my face, and I jump up, lifting my arms, and break into a blind run. But someone's shouting after me, shouting, 'Madman! Madman!' and I've left my bag behind, so I stop and turn, my arms still covering my face. It's the reading man who's shouting, and he's waving, and beckoning, and pointing at the floor between us. Totally freaked out, I peer down, and scream again, because it is the pigeon, dismembered, three pieces, the body and the two wings, flattened, and somehow blackened, lying on the blue speckled floor.

And then I see that it's my hat and my two gloves, which had been on my lap, and the reading man is leaning over to pick them up. The pigeon doesn't seem to be anywhere, so I lower my arms. 'Thank you!' I take them from him, but I drop one of the gloves again, and we both go for it, nearly knocking heads. He gets to it first. 'Thank you!' I say again, and he smiles, and his eyes crinkle. His book is called *The Heart Is a Lonely Hunter* by Carson McCullers. I've heard of it, but I've never read it. 'I thought it was the pigeon.' I really wanted to explain that last crazy scream. 'I thought these were . . .' I hold up my hat and gloves, thinking, he will *never* understand, that I should just pick up my bag and walk far away down the train. But the reading man is laughing, full of comedy, and empathy. 'Yes, yes!' he says. 'You thought I was pointing at the pigeon.'

'Yes, but I thought that *these* were the pigeon. I thought . . .'

'Hah!' He laughs louder, nodding, totally getting it, he thinks it's *hilarious*, and suddenly I'm laughing too. And the children are laughing, and their sad-eyed mother is smiling, and the celebrity has lifted his chin out of his scarf, and is grinning from ear to ear. And when I sit down, I see that the teenager is smiling, and I smile back at him, and he shakes his head, still smiling. And I just *love* him. I love everyone. Especially the reading man, who has gone back to his book, with a smile still playing on his lips. The pigeon is wandering about, inspecting the floor, such a filthy, decrepit bird. I love that bird. I love its hardiness. I love its self-containment. I love the actor, who is a *brilliant* actor, if *only* I could remember his name. And I am very fond of the children, and their mother, who is talking to them both, probably about me, and stroking the little boy's hair. And that cream soda woman. What amazing hair. What an amazing coat. What amazing eyelashes – great shelves of black, shadowing her neon-blue eyes. For the first time I notice an old Indian lady, an anorak over her sari, lots of shopping, battered Mary Janes. Her look is piercing, and I smile at her, and she doesn't smile back, but that's just her way, it's absolutely fine. The train has come out of the tunnel, and golden light is flooding in, and the reading man is reading aloud again, and though I still can't make out the words, it is so lovely, like I'm a child and he is reading me a bedtime story.

And the train arrives at Finchley Road, the actor stands up, the cream soda woman stands up; and the reading man stands up, stuffing his book in his pocket, and as he steps out of the train he turns and lifts his hand. I lift my hand back, smiling and smiling, but then I see that the pigeon is walking round and round a yellow pole. 'You need to get off, pigeon!' I cry. The bird is very dear to me now, and I really don't want it to be trapped on the train all the way to Wembley Park. 'It's not going to get off!' I point at it. 'Someone needs to . . .' But no one moves. So I get to my feet and move towards it, waving my arms, trying to herd it out. I'm bold, now, with the pigeon, I'm not fright-ened of it, I just want it to get off, but we run round and round the yellow pole like a couple of complete fools, and the reading man has stopped on the platform to watch. And then the beeping starts, meaning the doors are about to close, and I cry, 'Oh no!' I can't bear it. But at the very last second, the pigeon scurries between the doors and onto the platform, cool as a cucumber.

I watch the pigeon until I can't see it any more, and then I go and sit down. And that's when the Indian woman starts talking to me.

'No need to worry about the pigeon.' She's leaning forward, hands on her knees, shouting over the roar of the train. 'The pigeon doesn't worry about you. Why should you worry about the pigeon?' I shrug and smile, but I feel tense again. She's not really having a go at me, it's just her way, but I want to cry. I get out my phone. On the screen, my friend Chloe kisses her new boyfriend, who is from Quebec, and very cute. Yearning twists my guts.

3.

The Indian woman gets off at North Harrow. I look out at the mysterious suburbs: the boxy houses, the pyramid roofs, the satellite dishes; a flash of a park, flat and green, a pair of goalposts, a deserted play area. I feel the melancholy weight of them, and my stomach turns over. I blow my nose and think back to holding hands over Ruth Ellis's grave. How, when I finally escaped back to the warm belly of the city, it came to me that I wasn't seeing Paul Fildes to relieve my own loneliness, but to relieve his. I ghosted him. Autumn turned into winter. I went for long walks along the river, all the way into town, looking at the lights on the water, listening over and over to the 'Heart of Glass' mash-up from *The Handmaid's Tale*. And then one day he turned up on my doorstep. I hadn't even realized he knew my address. To begin with he was stiff and angry, saying that I owed him £200, and I said I was very sorry, and would pay him back within a week, if he would please give me his bank details. But then he sighed, and said, 'Poor Dido. You look awful. I knew you must be ill.' And for some reason this made my eyes fill up, and he did that thing of taking hold of my jaw, tipping my face up so he could see into it, and I clenched my teeth and shook his fingers off. And he stepped over the threshold, saying, 'Dido, Dido, why can't you bear anyone to look after you?' And one of the invisible humans came out of the kitchen to see what was going on, and I had to let him in, and up into my little room under the rafters, and it was like Alice when she ate the Eat Me cake, there just wasn't enough space for him. I was pathetic, mumbling that yes, I'd been depressed, and letting him explain to me about my trust issues. And then I let him hug me, and nuzzle at my neck. And it was all back on again, and coming up to Christmas. He hadn't made any plans, and was wondering if he could host his millennial waif. I would need to stay over on Christmas Eve because of the lack of transport. But he didn't want to rush me. He would sleep on the sofa. He paused, patting my knee, and then sighed, and said, 'At least think about it.'

I imagine what would happen if I succumbed to Paul Fildes. Waking up on Christmas morning together, naked between his nylon sheets, and he would kiss me, and call me his beautiful millennial. He would tell me there was no need to ever go back to the house in Mile End, and I would agree. I wouldn't be missed. Eventually the invisible humans would realize I had gone, and put my stuff into bin bags, and let the room to someone else, someone more able, more nimble, more 'London'. And I would become Mrs Fildes, and give the bungalow my feminine touch. I would no longer find him repellent, but would cleave to him, like a pet. I would look out onto the cul-de-sac, and, mid-afternoon, he might take a break from day trading to walk me around it. And when we got back in, I'd make us both a cup of tea.

4.

Trussed in navy Gore-Tex, he meets me off the train. 'Oh poor Dido,' he says. 'You're full of cold.' I'd been thinking we'd just go for a coffee, somewhere close to the station, but he wants to take me to a nice pub in Old Amersham. On the bus I go back to rehearsing the Christmas sentences in my head, but when I open my mouth I say that the most terrible thing happened on the train. I tell him about the pigeon, its deformed feet, and how I panicked in front of the other passengers. When I've finished he thinks for a while, biting his lip.

'You have told me that the pigeon terrified and repulsed you. Enough for you to lose control in front of strangers.' He shudders, and closes his eyes. I look out of the window, at a DIY shop called Chiltern Mica Hardware. 'It's about intimacy, isn't it?' He takes hold of my chin. 'Dido, is this your way of asking me to help you over your fear of intimacy?'

'No,' I say. 'I was telling you about a poor mangled pigeon, and how it freaked me out.' I get a flash of the reading man laughing, the crinkles round his eyes.

In the empty dining area of the pub a waitress is cleaning the tables with disinfectant so strong it makes my eyes itch. I can just hear Ed Sheeran and Beyoncé singing together on the radio in the kitchen. He buys two glasses of house red, and asks if it ever occurs to me to ask *him* a question. I think of the ballerina, but I ask him whether he is still in touch with Joy, his ex-girlfriend, and how she's getting on. He looks puzzled, as if he can't remember who she is, and then says that she's fine. 'What, better?' I ask, and he says that she's made a full recovery, and has gone travelling.

I get out the money.

'What's that for?' he says.

'It's what I owe you,' I say. 'It was kind of you to lend me it.'

'But you can't afford to pay me back. You're broke.'

'I'm OK. I'll manage.'

'I don't want it.' He pushes it back at me, panicked. I stare down at the wad of notes. 'Dido, please,' he says. 'If you really want to pay me back, then spend Christmas with me.'

'No,' I say.

'Why?' he says.

'Because I don't want to see you any more.'

I stand up, taking my coat off the back of my chair, and he tells me to sit back down, for goodness' sake. I say that I'm going, and he stands up too, and says he'll catch the bus with me. I say I'd prefer it if he didn't. When he tries to help me with my coat I push him away. The waitress looks over. He steps back.

'So you're paying me off,' he says.

'I'm paying you *back*,' I say.

'You're going off to be an escort.'

I look towards the door.

'Well, I hate to be the one to tell you, Dido, but you're probably not pretty enough.' He nods, emphatic. 'You're too scruffy. Too grubby-looking. And your hair, my love, is *terrible*.'

I smile and leave the pub, lighter of step, a burden lifted. The bus is there at the bus stop, and I'm stepping onto it when he catches me up. 'Have the blasted money, Dido.' He shoves it into my bag. I expect him to insist on getting on with me, but he stays on the pavement. 'I wish you well, Dido!' he cries. 'I wish you a long and happy life!' The bus pulls away. Feeling really bad again, I wave goodbye.

But then the relief of being back among those cheerful yellow poles, and seeing the word *ALDGATE* sliding along the black strips. I'd been out to the very edge of things, but now I'm travelling back, the enormous orange sun setting behind me. Packs of schoolkids get on, laughing, squabbling, shrieking, munching crisps. And then they're gone, and there's just the roar of the train, and it's dark, and the train is reflected in its own windows. The two women sitting next to me are going to do their Christmas shopping. One of them is going to buy Iconic Drops for

Misty, and an Amazon Echo for Ben. I think of the £200 in my bag, and whether I should tag along with them to Oxford Street, go on a spending spree; or whether to stuff it into the man at Aldgate's cup, and tell him he should take the tinsel off his poor dog. The track straightens, and I can see far along the train, all the way to where a white girl in gold baggy trousers is filming a black girl in a pink tutu doing gymnastics around a yellow pole. I think of the ballerina in the photograph, and her little monster, and it clutches my heart. Then the tutu girl goes into a backbend, hands gripping the pole, climbing downwards to the speckled floor. And I love the way London is so *itself*, so Londonish, and how everyone in it – lovers, loners, natives, settlers, fugitives, visitors, underdogs, fat cats – we are all part of its dance.

And at Finchley Road, the orange puffer jacket, the mop of black hair, and the book, sticking out of his pocket. When he sees me, he cries, 'Ha!' and looks around, lifting his hands in a question. I laugh, and shrug, and lift my hands too.

'You got rid of him in the end!' He shouts it over the beeping of the closing doors.

'Yes, I did.' I think of the pigeon's eyes, glassy orange buttons, and then of Paul Fildes's eyes, that violet intensity.

'It's for the best,' said the reading man. 'It was never

going to work out between you two.' And then, even though there are a few spare seats, he glances at my bag, and my heart lifts, and I lift my bag, and he sits down.

BAKERLOO

London Etiquette

Katy Mahood

Kilburn. Cyebourne. Place of iron-strong water. Where, centuries ago, polite company could find relief for stomach ailments – and for their baser urges, too. This morning, though, the clustered shopfronts that Anjoum passes show no sign of the dogfights and duels that once made this ancient roadway notorious. Daytime is creeping over the rooftops, their worn tiles sharpened by the backlight of a rising sun, as the bare strings of his guitar vibrate with every passing bus. His eyes fall to the stone that marks where the Kilburn Wells once stood. When he was a kid, his father loved to tell him about local history and the chalybeate water that drew the gentlefolk to the area. He's never worked out why his dad cared so much about this crappy corner of North West London. 'It's my home, that's why,' was the only explanation the old man would ever give.

Anjoum crosses the high road, heads down to the tube,

nodding to Jim in the ticket office, who raises his hand in a solemn greeting. The guitar strings twang as they tighten to tune. He starts to play.

Somewhere underneath this street, thinks William as his stiff legs carry him down the front steps, there is a river. The Westbourne. Running south from Hampstead through Kilburn, his adopted county. County Kilburn, where the voices came from all over – Cork, Kerry, Dublin, Ulster – a drop of the familiar that was more than welcome when he first arrived in London.

'Morning, Jim,' he says as he buys his ticket. Strange, he thinks, how an accent still shapes my words, even after all these years. Guitar music echoes against the walls. The ticket hall thrums with people, channelled untidily down the escalators to wait for the Bakerloo line. William makes the same journey each morning. Decades merge in every step. But today, he stops and steps out of the flow of commuters to listen to the busker stroke a seamless dance across the neck of his guitar. William reaches into his pocket. At the chink of the dropped coin the young man's eyes open. He smiles.

'Thank you, sir, much obliged.'

William nods. He stands a moment longer.

'Very nice,' he says as he steps back into the riptide of commuters, his mind sliding to the day ahead of him: the clinics, the consultations, the meeting this evening near to King's Cross.

The sky is bright by the time Anjoum leaves Kilburn Park. He checks his new digital watch as he strides along the high road: 9.27. *Hurry up*. Mum will already be visiting Dad at the hospital. She always takes the bus – says it's because it's cheaper, but he knows it's because she's scared. Perhaps you have to grow up with the tube to really get it, he thinks, as he lays his guitar on his bed and lifts the bag in the corner. At the front door he swears and spins back to his room. It's football tonight – up in Wood Green – nearly forgot. He pushes his kit on top of his books and jogs to the station, his bag still unzipped, willing the trains to be running on time. He doesn't want to be late for lectures again.

The clock in King's Cross says 19.29 as William walks towards the underground. He doesn't have the stamina these days that he once did, but he still plots his path with a Londoner's automation: face low, weaving through the gaps. The speed of this city. Motion is everywhere, bodies cross-hatch the concourse, trains roll into the platforms, pigeons scatter upwards as a guard blows his whistle. Even my body, thinks William, is a constant pulse of blood and breath and bacteria. Above the flurry of people he sees the shining roundel of the tube. The underground, he's always thought, is the city's saving grace; the only place where everyone is equal. Those young men with their braces and the rolls of banknotes in their pockets. Punks and tramps and Jehovah's Witnesses. All that restless difference, and yet London keeps on flowing with so much relentless life.

It still felt like there was a war on when he first arrived, a few years after the bombing had ended. He'd been shocked to see the urgent crowds, the smog-dense streets, the broken shells of bombed-out buildings. On the frantic wards of his first hospital job he'd found himself longing for the quiet of the university he'd left behind; the lamp-lit carrels in the library, where a dark-haired girl had tapped his shoulder and laughed at the words he was muttering as he'd memorized the bones in his hand. *Some Lovers Try Positions That They Can't Handle.* Naomi had been so quick to laugh in those days.

He buys an *Evening Standard* from the toothless man at his stand and rolls the paper under his arm. He hums as he moves, the tune he heard on his way to work this morning, played by the busker at Kilburn Park. The song has stayed with him all day. Now, in the throb of the crowded station, it is a soundtrack to the jostling travellers, to the plod of his feet and the ache in his shoulders. Below the departure board a group of nuns gather in a half-circle around their suitcases. People part around them, but these elderly ladies in their grey polyester jumpers take no notice. They stand there, unaware of how they are rupturing the flood of passengers, unaware of the laws of London etiquette: you must never stand still in a moving crowd. The display clicks as its letters rotate, updating the information about times and places and platforms. The clock on the board changes, too, as William watches: 19.33.

His feet fumble a clumsy quickstep down to the tube and he is engulfed by a sea of bodies moving. But he is oblivious now, halfway home already in his mind. This journey is his moment of transition, in which the city dissolves and his body is slowed once more to a singular pace. Years ago, he'd tried to explain it to Naomi, how it felt to be consumed by the city. How it felt to leave it all behind and become himself again. He remembers the hollow ache of exhaustion, his mind fizzing from the onslaught of so many new things to learn: patients and procedures and protocol. 'It's overwhelming. Like a lover with an appetite too vast to be sated.' Her green eyes had narrowed and her dark hair slipped from its pins as she shook her head at him and laughed. But he'd persisted, pressing her fingers to his neck. 'The city is alive, just like us – movement, heat and change—' She'd interrupted him with a kiss and carried on knitting, the wool trailing over her swollen belly, her cheeks flushed in the firelight. William stops walking for a moment and a young woman tuts as she sidesteps away. The cold fingers of the past close around him. *We would have made fine parents.* He takes one breath, then another. He pulls his ear, as he does at these moments, and the warmth of his flesh brings him back to the present. His eyes reach across to where the escalators send streams of people down to the depths of the platforms, over and again, their wooden tread softened by forty years of footfalls. Below them, machinery turns, its dull metal reflecting for a second the spark of a discarded match that has found its way into a crack.

Euston Road is bright with light and moving metal as Anjoum makes his way towards King's Cross, his bag banging heavily against his thigh. He can still smell the hospital, taste its decay and disinfectant in the back of his throat. In the roar of the traffic he pushes the afternoon away, a cacophony of images that he doesn't want to hold onto: sputum bowls and oxygen masks, the pitted sheen of his father's fingernails, yellowed against the bedsheet. He drops his empty packet of crisps, watching as it is lifted by a gust of fumes and absorbed into the city. He is glad not to be going straight home, glad of the few hours in Wood Green thinking of nothing but the game. Anjoum licks the salt from his fingers, feeling the wind bite his wet skin. He stuffs his hands into his pockets, clenching and releasing his fists to make the blood flow. A memory settles across him, softening the harsh November night: the sensation of his feet lifting from the ground, a kite above him, his father's cracked hands anchoring his middle. He holds his breath against the rush and noise of the busy road, trying to grip onto the remembered warmth of those hands as they held him safe.

Above the squat rise of the station the sky is starless, tainted orange by the city's sodium glow. Below, trains rumble in the dark. Anjoum feels the sudden tug of home, where his mother will be cooking pans of food that his father will never eat. She has grown so thin, her bright pink jumper swallows her whole, but she cooks and cooks, beading the kitchen windows with fragrant condensation: turmeric, cumin, coriander. He runs through the journey in his head, reciting the stations that he'll pass through on his way to Wood Green. He presses the light on his watch:

19.34. Head down, he walks in a fluid line, finding gaps as soon as they arise, swerving round a man who halts suddenly to consult a folded map. 'Watch out, mate,' he calls out as he passes – but he is too late to stop the inevitable collision. A furiously lacquered woman spits obscenities as the flustered man fumbles with his map and tries to move aside, buffeted by every passing traveller. Anjoum laughs. This place will eat you alive if you let it, he thinks, as he walks into the ticket hall and searches his pockets for his travelcard. London is a place you have to own – find its rhythm and make it yours. That's what he loves about the busking, the way you can change a person's day with a few simple chords. And it's a bit of money, on top of the student grant. God knows he and his mum need every penny just now. He pats the coins in his pocket from this morning: two pounds and thirty-six pence. Perhaps he'll call in at the shop on his way home after football, buy his mum some of that baklava that she loves and entice her to take a few bites. Since his dad's been in hospital she can barely eat at all. But she's always had such a sweet tooth, perhaps the syrup-drenched pastry might tempt her to try.

At the top of the escalator Anjoum eyes the metal bars that punctuate the smooth chute of the mid-section. He remembers sliding down them only a few years ago; can still feel the teenage thrill of breakneck speed and disapproval. His eyes are caught by a sudden rush opposite – a knot of people moving. The shout comes from the foot of the escalators; a policeman is waving people along from the platforms, up and out of the station. 'Keep going!' There is a charge in the air, a waft of smoke. The policeman's radio crackles, 'Escalator Four – evacuation underway.' His face grows red as his voice grows louder. 'Everyone out – now!' Commotion builds, the crowds no longer flow but thunder and Anjoum feels his body tighten. The escalators stop rolling and he turns on his heel, walking back up the steps he's just descended. He starts to hum – it's what he does when things feel edgy – and finds he is mouthing the song from this morning, the one he was playing when that man stopped to listen. Strange what pops into your head when you're nervous, he thinks. People begin to run, the air grows thin with panic. He quickens his step, moving with the singularity of the crowd, taking the hand of a woman beside him, whose face is twisted with terror. 'It's going to be all right,' he starts to say, but a swell of people behind push him onwards and his fingers slip from hers as he is forced faster up the steps.

I'm too old for this, thinks William as he struggles back from the platform, carried towards the exit by an accelerating crowd. A young woman clasps his arm and asks if he's all right, but he tells her to hurry ahead. 'Don't you worry about me, dear, I'm quite hardy. I lived through the war.' She smiles, relief lighting up her young face, and stutters, 'If you're sure?' even as she speeds ahead. William's breath is rasping in his chest as he climbs, his shoulders knocked by people running past him. There is a fierce surge as he reaches the top and a woman stops as a small child stumbles. William slows to help her, hoisting the compact body of the little girl in his arms and drawing on the last of his strength to press her to her mother. 'Go! Run!' he gasps and they do. He reaches out for the cool tile of the wall and leans against it. The air is growing hotter, he can feel that something is about to happen. His vision dims as the seething hall of people spins before him and he slides to the ground. The white numbers of the clock on the wall by the escalator turn over – 19.40. He closes his eyes.

Across the tangle of people running through the ticket hall, Anjoum sees a figure collapsed beside the wall. His lungs burn as he rushes over, pulling the man's arm around his shoulder and dragging him through the crowd. The man is breathing in quick, shallow rasps. 'Hang in there, fella,' Anjoum croaks. He feels the hammer blow of his heart against his chest and his own breath growing ragged. He knows they need to get out, but the old man is struggling to walk and doubt seizes Anjoum with a sudden hideous clarity. 'Come on!' he shouts, but he cannot do this alone. And then – from where he doesn't know – there is someone beside him. An arm is holding Anjoum up, an unseen strength is pulling them both along. The darkness swims with kites and sky and sirens and a voice that sounds like his father's. 'You're OK, kid – you done well – here you go now, I'll just set you both down here.' Far below, there is a hollow sound of air igniting. *Woomph*. Fire moves like water, a wave bursting from wood and varnish heated from the flames beneath, ripping through the station as a single hellish flash. The heat fuses the wires of the clock beside the escalator, which will forever be stuck at 19.45. People scramble like jetsam across the ticket hall, screams piercing through the clouds of dense black smoke.

William blinks. There is a wall behind him, orange light above. There is air. Dear God, the air! He sucks it in and feels it tracking to his lungs, sharp with cold but he doesn't care. He lifts his hand, soot-black beneath the street lights, miraculously unhurt. Traces the bones beneath the skin. Scaphoid. Lunate. Triquetrum. Pisiform.

Trapezium. Trapezoid. Capitate. Hamate. *Some Lovers Try Positions That They Can't Handle.* When he laughs, the young man lying next to him turns.

'You OK there?'

William can feel every nerve and pulse of his body, but his mouth won't form a word. *You saved my life*, he wants to say, as so many of his patients have said to him over the years. Until now he has never understood the power of those professional miracles he performs. He rubs his eyes as he tries to find the words and when he opens them he is looking at a face he swears he knows.

'It's you,' is all that he can manage.

Anjoum smiles. 'It is.'

William shakes his head. 'I mean, I know you. You're the busker.'

Anjoum looks again and sees the man from earlier, who'd listened as he played guitar. 'Oh—' he begins, but his voice leaves him. His throat has grown uncomfortably tight. William stretches out his hand and clasps the young man's arm as he pushes himself to his feet.

'Thank you.'

Anjoum nods. He stands and wipes his face, which flashes bright, then darkens as the blue lights turn beside them. On the other side of the cordon, firefighters run into the dark mouth of the station, their white helmets the last thing to be obscured by the smoke. William squints, his eyes still blurred with grit.

'So you're from Kilburn too, are you?'

Anjoum thinks of his music echoing against the dirty brown glaze of Kilburn Park station, of the pocket skyscraper under which he'd had his first kiss, of the high road that heaves with noise and life and history. The place his father loves. The place where he belongs.

'I am.'

'Fancy a walk? I'd be glad of the company.'

Tomorrow both men will realize the scale of the horror they have escaped. William will sit alongside Naomi at the breakfast table, newspaper spread before him, images of carnage made banal in black and white. Her hand will shake as she sets the dishes down. Anjoum will wake in the early hours and peer through the crack of his mother's bedroom door, watching her small frame curled around the space where his father should be. He will stare at the snowy television screen until the day's programmes begin and, when they do, guilt will burn across his body. *Why them and not me?* But for now, there are just these simple things: air and light and being alive. Anjoum looks at William and offers his arm.

They walk in silence, savouring the tang of fumes and the shriek of brakes as they move through the roaring engine of the city's heart, heading west along the Euston Road until they reach Regent's Park station. At the top of the brightly lit steps William pauses and leans against the gleaming green tiles. He shakes his head. 'I can't,' he says. Anjoum nods. He touches the old man's shoulder and they walk, cutting the corners of the Bakerloo line – Baker Street, Edgware Road, Maida Vale – seeking out the underground's bright beacon to show them the way home.

HAMMERSMITH & CITY

She Deserves It

Louisa Young

Autobiographical jewels of mine hang from that pink ribbon as it ambles across the city. Think of them as coloured light bulbs strung along frayed electric flex over a market stall; a long twist of Chinese lanterns glowing in the dusk; damp-stained gems of coloured diamanté dangling at intervals from a cheap foxed chain. A rosary of things that happened. The stations of the King's Cross to Hammersmith stretch.

Think of London lying naked by the river, wearing everything that is inflicted on her. Decorated, damaged, ignited, weighted, chained, wounded, loved, undermined, traversed, surviving.

Euston Square

Is where I was born. University College London Hospital. It was UCH then and my brother said it stood for United Cow Houses because I was a cow.

It's where you get the train to Wigan where my darling was from.

He called UCLH the Euston Hilton. We spent so much time there, with the radiotherapy (daily) and the chemo-therapy (weekly) and the insertion of the PEG tube and the nutritionists and the pain clinic and the surgeons and oncologists and CPEX tests and anaesthetists and the removal of his jawbone and half his tongue and the speech therapy and the no-more-eating and no-more-talking and all the things. The full-time job of love.

At the first appointment, when he was rushed from one expert to another to another, we were for a while in an oncology consulting room with little enamel panels on the window sills saying *Please do not throw cigarette ends out of this window*, which goes to show, something. Looking out I could see across the car park to the back of the building on Gower Street where I was born, on a trolley in the corridor, because I was the fifth child and I came quick.

When you're having radiotherapy at UCLH, you're two floors down in the basement, so the radioactivity is contained. 'We're under the northern end of Tottenham Court Road, by the lights,' a nurse said. 'Through that wall, that's the platform at Warren Street tube.'

Paddington

Is where I grew up, and where my child was born. It was the Central line that ran right under our house, making the strange and marvellous vibrations I could hear when I put my head underwater in the bath. It was the double-strand Circle-and-District lines that hid behind the fake frontage in the stucco terrace of Leinster Gardens, with its blind grey windows. You can see it from Porchester Terrace on the way to primary school (Hallfield Junior Mixed, sixty-eight languages spoken) if you climb up on the wall and look over. My sister made a beautiful swirling graffiti of the words 'Our Hearts Are Around Us' on that wall. You can almost see the ghost of the graffiti too. I can see it, of course. I will always see it. But Paddington is where all the strands tangle, the busy red and liquid beating heart, connected on all sides, the coming and the going. The coming of my only child: which took forever, and her father went so many times to the same café on Praed Street that he became a sweet joke with the proprietor, and in the end had free breakfasts. And the going of my own dear dad. The boats in the canal outside the window of the room he died in were like a list of memories of his life: one called Arthur like his grandson, one from Pewsey where his father had lived on the Kennet and Avon Canal he was named after, and the library boat, full of books.

He was in and out of that hospital like a weatherman.

Because of his dementia, one of us would spend the night on the floor. One night it was me. In the morning came the usual clattering and vicious lights, followed by, at about 6 a.m., our core family – seven or eight of them, led by my ghost-pale mother – gliding and crowding into the small room on a cloud of trepidation.

Dad greeted them cheerfully. I rose squinting from behind the bed.

A night nurse had turned two pages in the nurses' book, and rung Mum in the small hours and told her Dad was dead. But Dad was not dead. The man in the next room was dead, God rest his soul.

'Dad's Lazarus!' we cried, and sent the youngsters for coffee and were glad to be all together and wondered if there was a word for the opposite of disappointment, because that was the elation we were feeling.

A few years later he *did* die, in that same hospital. Again, I'd spent the night on his floor. 'What are you doing today?' he'd said. 'Going to the library,' I said. 'Going to write.'

'Good,' he said, and I went to the tube.

Hammersmith

Was secondary school. I did not like Miranda Brooks, because when someone asked what her father did she said, 'He's an accountant,' and I said, 'Is that a turf accountant?' because that was the only kind of accountant I knew about, having read the sign on the shopfront on Bishops Bridge Road every time I went to tea with Clare from Hallfield above the Royal Oak, which was where she lived.

'Certainly not,' she said. 'He's a *chartered* accountant.' I didn't know what that was any more than I knew what a turf accountant was, but I could tell when I was being put down all right.

Or being misinterpreted. Perhaps she thought I was being rude suggesting he was a turf accountant. Perhaps she knew what a turf accountant was. But then what was wrong with being a turf accountant anyway? I just liked being clear.

Also, because she tried to get Susan Rosen off me, and I liked Susan Rosen very much and did not care for the whole breaking friends and possessiveness aspect of being thirteen and a girl. And because when there was to be a school trip, and my parents said I could go, and Susan's parents said she could go, although it would be over Passover, and Miranda's parents said she couldn't go, *because* it was Passover, and I was glad and wrote in my diary that I was glad Miranda couldn't go, and it was because of Passover, Tatty Naradnic stole my diary from my locker while we were changing for netball and wouldn't give it back and read it out loud and told everybody I was anti-Semitic because of what I'd said about Miranda. I didn't know the word syllogism yet and even if I had I wouldn't have wanted to use it because I was self-conscious about my lisp, but now I didn't like Tatty either, because she had slandered me by warping information from a stolen source, then some other girls said I didn't like Tatty because I was jealous of her big bosoms and pretty face, so I said what logic does a girl have to have here, she stole my fucking diary and misrepresented me. They looked pitying. I felt I was on a losing wicket in this place.

A few years later I left my schoolbag on the seat outside the dining hall during lunch, which gave the deputy head (notorious for the velvet-soled slippers which allowed her to pad around the place catching people out) a reason to take it away and look inside it, which was apparently permissible. She called me in to her office and it turned out that she too had read my diary – a little one, the 'what you're doing on Wednesday' type, not the 'here is why I hate Miranda Brooks' type. She had found several week-night engagements and also a little packet of rolling tobacco. 'St Saviour's girls do not smoke,' she announced, a splendid presentation of dishonesty and wishful thinking. And, 'You go out too much during the week.' I think I said – I hope I said – that this was my business and my parents', that this was not a boarding school, that she could do one. I don't remember. I just remember burning injustice.

There was a shoplifting period: go to Biba, dimly lit, ostrich-feathered, sparkly Biba; steal as much as you could on the way up to the Rainbow Room, the restaurant on the top floor, go and compare booty in the loos, and then, on the way down again, put it all back. That was the harder skill. The school called the whole year in and told us they knew who was doing it, and if they confessed of their own accord they would not be in trouble. As if anyone would fall for that! But of course one or two went in and said, 'It wasn't me but I know it was x, y and z.'

Later Anjelica Huston wrote that Barbara Hulanicki, the owner of Biba, said she didn't mind the teenagers shoplifting because it meant the coolest girls in London were wearing Biba clothes and it was great advertising.

Someone had an essay to finish; if she didn't get it in she'd be in trouble, if she was in any more trouble her parents were taking her away and sending her to finishing school. She was in the local library struggling with the essay; and her friend got someone's boyfriend to ring in and say there was a bomb. (This was the Seventies; bomb scares and bombs were normal to us London children, because

Oliver Cromwell had put different types of Christian on top of each other in Ireland in the seventeenth century, and the 'love thy neighbour' bit had got lost in the ensuing historical melee. Tube stations closed, Harrods, Hyde Park. At home we'd go to the back of the kitchen, away from the road, and someone would say 'Is it like the Blitz?' and our parents would say 'No.')

We were all filed out onto the netball courts, glad of the change of scene. She finished her essay. Her parents took her out of school anyway because they discovered she was going out with Susan Rosen's brother, and the Rosens were not rich or grand in any way, unlike this girl's family.

Many years later I met a man who had just come out of prison after serving five years for a false bomb scare. He said he hadn't done it. He was trying to rebuild his life, as an ex-convict. The shame burned, on behalf of those girls, that world.

If you got into Oxford or Cambridge from that school they engraved your name on the wall in gold. I wanted to do well but I didn't want my name on their wall. Dilemma. Only not. I'd been leaving since the day I arrived.

And Hammersmith is Charing Cross Hospital. Scene of the death of my darling. When they knock the hospital down and replace it with overpriced housing, all the death scenes will be floating in empty air, way up high where the skeins of geese fly down at dusk to the reservoirs at Barn Elms. Perhaps those empty blocks of air have already been defined and divided to be sold. Later, they'll be someone's prestigious bathroom, or someone's really not affordable lounge. Or a logistical solution to a corrupt foreign bureaucrat's where-to-store-his-bribes problem. Or a bankrupt property developer's death blast, as the bubble holding them up contracts, expands, explodes, disappears.

Ladbroke Grove

Was where I went to help my sister paint murals in the bays under the Westway, the new motorway across North Kensington, a place of great brutality and ugliness. The North Kensington Amenity Trust ran a job creation scheme for unemployed youth, and it was to be part of that. She raised funds from charities, got free paint from manufacturers, rented a scaffolding tower. She wanted to make the city more beautiful and started there, covering the concrete with blue sky, stylized clouds, green hills, and massive painted caryatids with rainbow outlines, supporting the flyover. She was bringing beauty to a problematic place.

She started doing it on her own, and the youth turned up, or not, day by day, to help her. It was painting by numbers: red, white, green, yellow and blue; 1, 2, 3, 4, 5. Mainly blue. I recall being up ladders, in dungarees.

Frestonia was going on. Ladbroke Grove was Portobello was freedom. I had a crush on Pete the Plumber: waist-length red hair; bare chest, chopper bike. The stucco palaces of Elgin Crescent and Blenheim Crescent were full of squats and impoverished intellectuals. We'd climb into the communal gardens and lurch from house to house eating everything in each other's mothers' fridges. Mothers couldn't bear waste because of the war. We'd sit on the roofs and sing 'Maybe the Last Time' in harmony, in Forties tea dresses from the market, and Doc Martens. I was doing my A Levels that year.

She stopped doing the murals when she got pregnant. Later the bays were filled in; the murals remain, somewhere behind the gym and the shopping arcade. I still dream of my sister's clouds, the blue and white.

St Pancras

Here's Old St Pancras Church, with the high graveyard behind its blackened wall. One of my first jobs was going round London looking at old churches, to update the book about them my parents wrote in the Fifties. If you were a dentist on Harley Street this was where the tomb raiders would get the nice new teeth you needed for your wealthy clients; other parts also available. And in the 1860s, when the Midland Railway was built (north of Euston Road, because the aristocratic owners of everything further south weren't having any of this industrial stuff going on on their land, thank you), it was the bodies of Old St Pancras that had to be shifted, and it was the job of the architect's young assistant, Thomas Hardy, future novelist and poet, to dismantle those tombs and move those corpses. There stands, still, an ash tree bearing his name, surrounded and wedged by the mossy, propped-up gravestones of the dead who he disappeared.

And here's the phenomenal hotel at St Pancras, now righteously called the Renaissance. Originally it only had about four bathrooms to its hundreds of bedrooms. It was one of the last to be built for pitchers and ewers and servants: the original hot and cold running water. When the whole massive Victorian caboodle, station and hotel, was to be demolished in the Sixties, among those who came to its rescue was my dad, working then as a junior minister in the Ministry of Housing and Local Government, who quietly, conscientiously and repeatedly mislaid and bungled the planning applications for demolition, until that decade's mania for destruction passed. I look up at it and think: survivor.

Shepherd's Bush Market

Is where I live. Up till a few years ago it was called just Shepherd's Bush, the same as the other station four blocks along which is completely separate and serves two other lines.

I was walking up there recently on my way to the British Library where I go to write, the heels of my boots clacking along briskly. Feeling good. Outside one of the newsagent's my ankle turned briefly – I recovered it in the same movement, not a problem. I continued along. I was going to be writing this: Hammersmith & City. The pinky mauve ribbon (Pantone 197) round my city's body, from which my scenes hang.

After a few moments I noticed a little voice behind my right shoulder, singing, very quietly.

I was pleased! I often sing under my breath. My friends have warned me about it. The word eccentric has been used. But I'm a songwriter. I sing melodies into my phone late at night as I stride home.

This was not a beautiful melody, though. It was a whiney, dirgey little three-note tune, on a falling note. Borderline 'nyah na na nyah na'. It went:

'She   de-   She   de-
   fell, she   served   fell, she   served
           it;   it;

'She   de-   She   de-
   fell, she   served   fell, she   served
           it;   it.'

My curiosity was piqued. But I didn't care to give the crooner the dignity of a glance over my shoulder. After a few more bars of walking, I just slowed down and fell back.

Ha! She fell silent immediately. So she has some shame.

I slid my eyes towards her. She was a schoolgirl, perhaps thirteen years old, in an ordinary blue school uniform, with school badge, and instead of a school hat a tight blue hijab.

I walked behind her shoulder, as she had walked behind mine. We were clearly both heading to the station. I had time.

I picked up her tuneless tune, almost under my breath.

'She fell, she deserved it,' I droned quietly. 'She fell, she deserved it; she fell, she deserved it.'

No response.

I drew closer to her, feeling naughty.

'That's a pretty little song,' I said, as if to nobody.

She glanced across at me, eyes low. I didn't look at her.

'Did you make it up?' I said, again asking the damp air and the grey pavement.

'It's about you!' she said suddenly, eyes flashing, spiteful. I got a sudden clear glimpse of her with her parents, being told off: the being squashed, the sullen resentfulness, the outbursts, the punishment, the whole ungodly cycle of the repression of a bumptious child.

'I thought it might have been!' I said, as if complimented. She walked on.

'But it's not really true, is it?' I said. I think about the relation between truth and art quite a lot. How art uses forms and structures to make it clearer, tidier, more comprehensible. Fiction, unlike reality, has to be believable. Also, how much of someone else's truth are you allowed to use in your writing or your song before you become a thief of their life?

'Because I didn't fall, did I?' I said. 'I sort of semi-stumbled, and then righted myself. But apart from you putting an indignity on me which didn't actually happen,' I continued, 'I'm interested in why you feel that a person would deserve to fall. Why do you think that I deserved to fall?'

She didn't break her rhythm.

'And also,' I said conversationally, because this was interesting, 'why the emphasis on "she"? *She* fell, *she* deserved it. Do you feel that women deserve to fall?'

She still didn't break rhythm, but she looked at me, straight. 'High heels!' she said, with considerable scorn.

I heard the heels of my boots clack alongside her, and saw the argument branch out in two definite separate lines, neither of which I cared to give up in favour of the other.

On the one hand, the boots were not high, by any standard, so that was factually incorrect. (Another branch popped out: what would you classify as high? To you, perhaps my heels are high. But a great many much higher heels are visible on feet, pages, adverts and screens all around us. My boots are simply and mathematically lower. One inch, perhaps, where you see six inches or seven smoking outside nightclubs and lounging across posters all across town.)

On the other, original second branch, hand, why would someone deserve to fall, for wearing high heels?

I had hoped that speaking to her would clarify the situation, but this young girl was becoming more possibilities, not fewer. Initially, I had thought: a little dim, disinhibited, perhaps a person with special needs? Or: spiteful teenage gal, no respect? Now I added to this list: victim of extremist religious teaching re female attire, even seeing an inch of heel on a winter boot as a crime deserving of the physical (and symbolic?) punishment of a fall.

It is serious, when a woman falls. Her virtue, dignity and her honour are lost. She has sought that which is forbidden to her kind, eaten of the fruit, disobeyed God, deviated from societal morality, sold her body for money, for her survival, or that of her children. She is a pariah. 'The once fall'n woman must for ever fall.' She deserved it.

'They're hardly high at all,' I said. 'They're just about high enough to keep my feet out of a puddle.' There were plenty of puddles about.

'You'll fall in a puddle and get your feet wet and you'll get tuberculosis and cancer and you'll DIE and you'll deserve it,' she cried at me gleefully – and nimbly diverted herself into the safety of a fried-chicken shop.

Hm.

As she went, because I do believe in educating young people, I called after her, 'You're more likely to die prematurely from eating fast food than from wearing high heels! Footwear doesn't give you cancer!'

Plus I remain deeply allergic to a schoolgirl bitch bully. Just because I'm grown up now doesn't mean I don't remember.

'Plus,' I yelled, 'everybody dies!'

Westbourne Park

Was the old Great Western Studios in the disused lost property office, where the artists had their studios. My sister's was on the actual disused platform, sheltered from the weather by the building above, because she carved such grand, huge pieces of marble you couldn't fit them inside a studio. From the train you'd see the Portakabin where she made tea and did the paperwork, and the big olive trees in pots that sheltered her and her work, and the marble torsos and massive angels' heads, a quick glimpse between the shimmering concrete-coloured olive leaves, as the train whooshed by.

The old studios were knocked down a while ago. You can see the new ones further along the Harrow Road, in a new building; like so much of the new London over which we old Londoners sorrow, it is glassy, fancy, and far too expensive for the people we were told it was to be for.

There was a bomb left at Westbourne Park station, in 1913. They think it was suffragettes.

King's Cross

Every day for years, Shepherd's Bush to King's Cross. Pick up a paper (copy of the *Metro*, lately: lovestruck column, celebrities I don't care about, couple of whacky news stories, Good News Feed – hurray, human beings are nice really). An invisible wave to my sister on the platform where she no longer is, as we pass. Then tuck the paper behind me and clear my mind: drop my shoulders, hum a little inside my head, moving back towards writingland; the imaginary landscapes, the non-existent people, the fields of research, the streams of thought, the slopes to climb, the chasms to investigate.

Decant at King's Cross. My, how it's changed over the many, many years. I wasn't there for the Nazi bombs that damaged the Metropolitan line (as the H&C was still called in 1941), but I remember the fire (1987); I remember the bombings (2005), and then again when some bastard failed to blow up Shepherd's Bush station, in the aftermath. I look at everybody on the train and think how close they might be to tragedy: the sleeping night-workers going home; the Muslim boy looking scared that someone's looking funny at his rucksack; the woman with tears so close behind her eyes you can see them. The Albanian buskers, the dogs, the drunks, the person practising their pole-dancing. Every person with a life as full and complex, as rewarding and as terrifying, as my own. Hello, human beings of London. I love you I hate you get your armpit off my face.

Because I am a regular and canny I have tricks for claiming my preferred seat while others are still learning that they have to give in their coat and actually sir that bag is too big and not transparent. I have a transparent bag already:

a sturdy, transparent, over-the-shoulder messenger bag that they gave my darling when he was on crutches. He's been dead six years now; the bag is still going strong. I've had it so long sometimes even members of staff at the Library don't know it's a Library-issue authorized transparent bag.

Off to the café, back to the reading room, sit, work. Work work work. Read read read. Write write write.

For years this has been my self-inflicted commute, my equivalent of whichever artist it was who every morning walked out of his front door in coat and hat, round the block and back in again to go upstairs to his studio. The psychological journey from relax to work. It is my only office.

Evening Standard on the way back; the daily tiny prayer for a seat.

I have written so many books in here. Seven? Eight?

This is where I took the call about his surgery.

Home from bloody home. Here I am now.

Further east

The chain holds fewer jewels of mine. Only the beautiful little old churches, sitting there still, Christ Church Spitalfields, St Mary-le-Bow, St Botolph's, St

Margaret Pattens, timeless and humiliated by giant plate glass and capitalism, all the things this old Londoner hates. The size of the new temples to profiteering, the sheer bloody number and ugliness. The lingering emptiness of the Gherkin. Nothing is good enough; everything must be changed, even the thing that arrived five minutes ago; everything must be sold and sold again, because the once fall'n woman is for ever fallen. Because in every change there's money to be made. No speck of land can exist in this city now unless it is being squeezed for as much money as it can possibly be squeezed for. And guess what? That kills it. My city is dying on me. Who will ever buy her back?

I never went east of Kingsway till I was twenty-three, seeking out the old churches for my mum and dad. There was no call. East London was a different country. At St Dunstan's Stepney Green, I saw and promised to remember the gravestone of Betsey Harris, who died suddenly while contemplating the beauties of the moon, in her twenty-third year.

Someone's solved religion, by the way. It's simple: treat it like a penis. Great that you have one, lovely that you're proud of it, but keep it to yourself and please don't shove it down the throats of children.

And now?

OK, look. Tonight, I'll go east instead. I'll just go. See the other end of the city; her lives and deaths. See how the young girls are, contemplating the moon, tripping over flagstones. Did Betsey sing in the street, or steal from shops? Do spiteful serenading maidens hold up motorways, or contemplate the moon? Who carves the names on gravestones? Have we learned kindness yet?

I'll check the light bulbs; try to handle each gem gently, to sing a sweeter song. She deserves it.

NOTES ON THE CONTRIBUTORS

JAMES SMYTHE is an award-winning writer of eight novels for adults, and three for young adults. He also writes for television and film. He lives in Worthing with his family. His most recent novel *The Ends*, was published in 2022.

MATTHEW PLAMPIN completed a PhD at the Courtauld Institute of Art and now lectures on nineteenth-century art and architecture. He is the author of five novels, *The Street Philosopher*, *The Devil's Acre*, *Illumination*, *Will & Tom* and *Mrs Whistler*. He lives in London with his family.

JOANNA CANNON graduated from Leicester Medical School and worked as a hospital doctor, before specialising in psychiatry. She is the author of *The Trouble with Goats and Sheep*, *Three Things About Elsie* and *A Tidy Ending*, published in 2022. Her memoir *Breaking & Mending*, a junior doctor's stories of compassion and burnout was published in 2019 and she is the editor of *Will You Read This Please?*, a collection of stories about mental illness, out in 2023. She lives in the Peak District with her family and her dog.

LIONEL SHRIVER is the author of fourteen novels including the National Book Award finalist *So Much For That*, the *New York Times* bestseller *The Post-Birthday World*, the *Sunday Times* bestseller *The Mandibles: A Family 2029–2047*, and the international bestseller *We Need to Talk About Kevin*. Her journalism has appeared in the *New York Times*, the *Guardian* and many other publications. Her short fiction has appeared in the *New Yorker* and her 2018 collection *Property*. Her first essay collection *Abominations* will be published in 2022. In 2014 she won the BBC National Short Story Award. She lives in London and Brooklyn, New York.

KAT GORDON read English at Somerville College, Oxford, and worked at *Time Out* briefly after graduating. She travelled extensively in East Africa where she also worked as a teacher and HIV counsellor. She received a distinction for her MA in Creative Writing from Royal Holloway and her debut, *The Artificial Anatomy of Parks*, was published in 2015, followed by *An Unsuitable Woman* in 2017. She lives in London with her partner and young son.

JOE MUNGO REED was born in London and raised in Gloucestershire. He has a degree in Politics and Philosophy from the University of Edinburgh and an MFA in Creative Writing from Syracuse University. His short stories have appeared in *VQR* and *Gigantic*, and his debut novel *We Begin Our Ascent* was published in 2018. He lives in Edinburgh.

TYLER KEEVIL grew up in Vancouver and in his mid-twenties moved to Wales. He writes novels, short stories, and non-fiction and has received a number of awards for his writing, including the *Missouri Review*'s Jeffrey E. Smith Editor's Prize and The Writers' Trust of Canada/McClelland & Stewart Journey Prize. He lectures in Creative Writing at Cardiff University.

LAYLA ALAMMAR grew up in Kuwait with an American mother and a Kuwaiti father. She has a master's in Creative Writing from the University of Edinburgh. Her work has appeared in the *Evening Standard*, *Quail Bell* Magazine and *Aesthetica* Magazine, where she was a finalist for the Creative Writing Award 2015. Her debut novel *The Pact We Made* was longlisted for The Authors' Club Best First Novel Award. Her latest novel is *Silence is a Sense*.

JANICE PARIAT'S debut collection of short stories, *Boats on Land* (2012), won her the Sahitya Akademi Young Writer Award

2013 and a Crossword Book Award for Fiction. Her first novel, *Seahorse*, was published in 2014 and was shortlisted for The Hindu Prize for Literature 2015. She has lived in London and Brighton and is currently based in New Delhi. Her latest novel is *Everything the Light Touches*.

TAMSIN GREY grew up in England and Zambia. She has worked as a cucumber picker, a yoga teacher, an oral historian, and as speechwriter to a secretary of state. 'Her Beautiful Millennial', which features in this collection, was shortlisted for the BBC National Short Story Award in 2019. *She's Not There* is her first novel.

KATY MAHOOD was born in 1978 and studied at Edinburgh and Oxford Universities. After a brief career in publishing, she has since worked in marketing, most recently for the cancer charity Maggie's. She has contributed to a number of publications on architecture and health and writes a blog which features occasional poetry and short fiction. She lives in Bristol with her husband and two children. *Entanglement* is her first novel.

LOUISA YOUNG was born in London and read history at Cambridge. She co-wrote the *Lionboy* series with her daughter, and is the author of ten further books including the bestselling *My Dear I Wanted to Tell You* – which was shortlisted for the Costa Novel

Award, and was a Richard and Judy Book Club choice – and its acclaimed sequels, *The Heroes' Welcome* and *Devotion*. Her memoir *You Left Early: A True Story of Love and Alcohol* was published in 2018, and her latest novel is *Twelve Months and a Day*. Her work is published in 36 languages. She lives in London.

ACKNOWLEDGEMENTS

With many thanks to the *Evening Standard*, Transport for London, every author who has contributed to this collection, and particularly to the many people who work on the Underground, and those who take it every day. These tales are for you.